JIM ANTHONY
SUPER-DETECTIVE

Airship 27 Productions

TM

Jim Anthony: Super-Detective Volume One
© 2009 Airship 27 Productions
www.airship27.com
Airship27Hangar.com

A Spicy Savage © copyright 2009 Norman Hamilton
Dawn Of The Purple Hoods © copyright 2009 Robert E. Kennedy
Death Walks Behind You © copyright 2009 Andrew Salmon
Curse of the Red Jaguar © copyright 2009 B.C. Bell

Interior llustrations © 2009 Pedro Cruz
Cover illustration © 2009 Chad Hardin

Editor: Ron Fortier
Associate Editor: Charles Saunders
Production and design by Rob Davis.

ISBN: 978-1-953589-63-7
Printed in the United States of America

Second Edition-

1 2 3 4 5 6 7 8 9 0

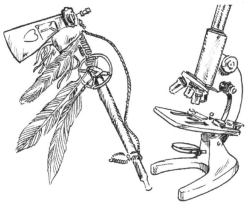

A SPICY SAVAGE

By Norman Hamilton

Perhaps the most outlandish pulp publisher of them all was Culture Publications. By the early 1930s there were many pulp titles that catered in one fashion or another to prurient taste. The adage that sex sells couldn't have been more obvious and as more and more publishers entered the market, that rule of thumb simply could not be ignored. In 1932, brothers Harry and Irwin Donenfeld acquired Pep, La Paree and Spicy Stories after the original publisher, Frank Armer, went bankrupt. They soon became the first titles of the DM Publishing (Donenfeld Magazines.)

The Donenfelds, not wanting to lose his contacts and experience, hired Armer to edit for them starting with *Super Detective*. It should be noted that this magazine featured a comic strip called *Betty Blake*. Armer was a proponent of comics and would incorporate them in most of the pulps he was involved with. Eventually, Harry Donenfeld and Armer agreed to start a new publishing venture called Culture Publishing to specifically print "spicy" fiction. These would be the standard crime/ mystery stories only with overt erotic underpinnings. The duo hired Kenneth Hutchinson as the Managing Editor of the "spicy" line.

Their first title dated July 1934 was SPICY DETECTIVE STORIES. It would soon be followed by SPICY ADVENTURE STORIES and SPICY MYSTERY STORIES. Two years later they would add SPICY HOLLYWOOD STORIES and even a SPICY WESTERN STORIES. Regardless of the genre, their covers featured beautiful young women skimpily clad while frantically trying to escape the clutches of some horrific impending doom.

Culture Publications would never achieve the success of their competitors but between the years of 1934 and 1946 they did a healthy business. Their most popular, long-lasting title being DAN TURNER, HOLLYWOOD DETECTIVE. Eventually conservative-minded church and civic groups began protesting the flagrant use of sex and by 1942 the company had dropped all its "spicy" titles when it then became Trojan Publishing. Although things tamed down a wee bit, keep in mind these were the same people running the show and any title they published still exploited sex and violence.

All the while publishers like Culture/Trojan were scrambling daily to make a profit in an overcrowded market, Street & Smith, the industry giant, continued to produce the biggest selling monthlies of them all, THE SHADOW AND DOC

SAVAGE. As expected, several of these cut-rate outfits attempted to copy them by creating mirror-like heroes of their own and Donenfeld and Armer were no different. Between them, and Ken Hutchinson, the idea was born to produce a Doc Savage rip-off who would be a brilliant superman, known throughout the world for his scientific breakthroughs. Like Savage he would have a New York headquarters and surround himself with a handful of special, unique aides. The difference would be in his personality. Unlike the stoic, near emotionless Clark Savage, Jr., this new fellow would be a man of hot-blooded passions, capable of flying into a fiery rage from the least provocation while at the same time having an appreciative eye for the fairer sex. In other words, he would be a sexy Doc Savage.

Super Detective would be the venue for this new, all American, red-blooded pulp hero, Jim Anthony. He would appear in the magazine from 1940 to 1942 in a total of twenty-five stories. Eventually the title would be altered to read: JIM ANTHONY – *Super Detective*. The son of an Irish adventurer, his mother was a Native American princess of the Comanche tribe. He was a scientific genius; inventor, research engineer, aerodynamics expert, art collector, adventurer, philanthropist; champion athlete, world famous criminologist, and chemist. He even resembled the Man of Bronze and was said to have the body of Greek God.

Aiding Anthony in his war on crime were a handful of close allies. Tom Gentry, a hulking, battered, freckled red-head, Irishman, he was Anthony's chief pilot, chauffeur, trained agent and best pal. Dawkins was Anthony's butler and kept his penthouse suite atop the Waldorf-Anthony spotless. But the strangest of this close knit group was Anthony's maternal grandfather, the Comanche medicine man, Mephito. The old man was well versed in Native American spirit lore and a true mentor to the often times impulsive Anthony.

Now, as stated above, Jim, unlike Doc, did like women and they certainly liked him. All kinds of femme fatales peppered his adventures. Many pulp fans are critical of this repeating thread throughout the early episodes, claiming they diluted the suspense and action of the tales and often times skirted the edges of soft pornography. Eventually one particular young woman arrived to take on the role of Anthony's primary love interest and she was Delores Colquitt, the daughter of Senator Colquitt. A blond, she had a slim shape, clear skin, taller than average and sparkling blue eyes. In the later stories she and Jim became engaged, thus ending his romantic escapades, much to the delight of his readers.

During the course of his short literary life, Jim Anthony battled several would be world conquerors, but his most tenacious foe was one Rado Ruric, who appeared in three stories. Ruric was the head of a group dedicated to the overthrow of the government and Anthony fought him in such places as Tibet, Mexico, Central America and the U.S.

Now, many long years after his last appearance, Jim Anthony, Super Detective is back in three brand new adventures thanks to *Airship 27 Prod*. During his original run, the character never seemed to find his proper place. He began as a clone of another hero and when that didn't work, his editors and writers attempted to morph him into a more down-to-earth detective character. Neither approach realized the genuine potential inherent in the series and thus it floundered as a pulp oddity. Not so with this new, improved Jim Anthony. Here he appears full blown as the true pulp hero he was always intended to be, clearly his own character full of possibilities. Roberts, Salmon and Bell have whipped up three terrific yarns that will have you applauding Jim Anthony's return and clamoring for more; much more. There's also some added historical data provided by Bell as an epilogue to his story that will round out what I've related here. I purposely opted not to repeat that material in this informal introduction.

We end with a rousing bravo to cover painter, Chad Hardin, whose magnificent image here pays homage to the classic *Super Detective* covers, with our hero's naked physique on the display for all the world to admire. And of course there's that scantily clad damsel in distress. Thank God, some things never change.

JIM ANTHONY

"SUPER-
-DETECTIVE"

JIM ANTHONY

in

Dawn Of The Purple Hoods

By Erwin K. Roberts

To all outward appearances the tall man in the custom tailored tuxedo seemed cool, calm, and collected. In reality, under his raven black hair, his mind roiled with frustration. He wanted desperately to be anywhere but in the gaily decked out hotel ballroom. Not that he wanted anything untoward to happen. The charity benefiting from the soirée helped untold numbers of people in need. The event just happened to be the capstone of a totally frustrating week. His face managed to maintain its easy going smile, just barely.

Then Jimmy Durante, the master of ceremonies, proclaimed, "The Sentinel chain of newspapers and magazines has raised a lot of money for The Salvation Army tonight, thanks to your generous donations. The silent auction closed while we sold an evening with the young new publisher. We will have those results momentarily. While we wait, we'll try to top our last auction. Ladies, now up for bid, an evening on the town, including Broadway show, dinner, and dancing, with one of the most eligible bachelors in the city. No! In the nation! He's over six foot tall. Charles Atlas seems a bit peaked standing next to him. He's a scientist, a solver of mysteries, and recently became publisher of one of the Sentinel's most prestigious competitors. Ladies, please give a warm welcome to Mr. Jim Anthony."

Trying not to blush, Jim Anthony stepped from the crowd to join Durante on the stage. Most of the audience clapped, but a couple of strident wolf whistles added laughter to the applause. Then came a few gasps as one of the energetic whistlers' evening gown almost took leave of her upper body.

"Whatcha think of the introduction?" asked Durante out of the side of his mouth.

"Good, but the reaction was even better," replied Jim with the first genuine smile on his lips in in three days.

Still waiting for the audience to quiet down, the comedian continued, "You think those female wolves'll win the bidding?"

"The one who held on to the top of her gown is the closest thing I have to a 'girlfriend.' She'll only bid to jack up the charity price. I think I recognize the one with the red face. If I'm right, she doesn't have nearly the deepest pockets in the bidding pool. We'll see."

The bidding got off to a lively start in fifty dollar jumps. Jim surveyed the audience. When the bid reached twenty-five hundred dollars a woman of about fifty called out,

"I'll double that bid!"

"Why thank you, ma'am!" exclaimed Durante. The host's head did a double take as Jim Anthony's voice seemed to pop directly into his ear while the big man's lips did not move.

"That's Mrs. Stubbing. She's standing next to her husband!"

"Am I correct? We have a bid of five thousand dollars from... Is it Mrs. Stubbing?"

The older lady didn't bat an eye. "That is correct. I'm bidding in the name of my daughter who is in graduate school."

"Oh my," exclaimed Durante with a slightly befuddled expression, "I sure wisht I had a mama like you! Are there any other bids? No other bids? Going once. Going twice! SOLD! One evening on the town with Señor Jim (love that name) Anthony goes to Miss Stubbing."

A few days later Marinda Stubbing unpacked her light travel case at her parents' small "in town" apartment. As she tried to decide what to wear for her surprise "birthday present" date she felt both nervous and very excited. She had almost told her mother that she had wasted her money. Then she looked a little closer at the engraved invitation. Jim Anthony! Of all people.

The apartment doorbell rang. Through the peephole she saw a good looking blonde smiling at her. Marinda blinked for a moment. The face looked familiar to her. Then she made the connection. Senator Colquitt's daughter. Wasn't she supposed to be... Oh, my!

Marinda decided to meet the issue, whatever exactly it turned out to be, head on. She opened the door saying, "Hello. Delores, isn't it?"

"That's right. I came to see you before your big date tonight."

"I've heard it said that you and Jim Anthony have been 'an item,'" replied Marinda. "I hope you don't think I'm deliberately poaching..."

"I haven't got an exclusive with the big lug. The way he sees things, no woman ever should. Too dangerous. In his opinion, anyway." Delores paused before continuing, "I asked around 'cause I couldn't remember ever hearing about you attending any kind of social event. Everybody says your nose never gets any sun for all the books covering it. I can't say if that's true, but I sure don't want the Big Boy Scout accused of mercy dating. If you're going to be my competition, even just for one evening, I want you to be worthy competition. Now, what kind of evening gown do you have?"

In the early evening of the day following the big charity date Delores wandered into Jim Anthony's laboratory in the penthouse of the Waldorf-Anthony Hotel. She wanted to hear all about what went on. She walked around an unfamiliar screen.

Delores stopped dead in her tracks. On a hospital bed lay Marinda Stubbing. Covered by a sheet so thin Delores could tell that she wore little or nothing under it. Wires ran from her forehead, from within her auburn hair, and upper chest, while tubes ran into both of her arms.

Marinda smiled through pale lips saying softly, "I must look quite the sight. I'm groggy and I feel like I'm roasting. But, Jim and two doctors tell me I'll be fine."

Not often caught completely off guard, Delores managed to stammer only, "What? How? Why are you here? And alone?"

"My nurse will be back in just a moment," replied Marinda with a thin smile. "I'll get to what happened in a moment. But first I wanted to thank you for your help. We had a wonderful time. At least I sure did. We ate at a terrific Chinese place. Saw Lunt and Fontanne in Giradoux's Amphytrion 38 at the Schubert Theater. And we danced until after one o'clock. He was so nice. And he can really talk about my field of study."

"I don't think I ever heard just what that is," said Delores.

"That's one of my big problems. My parents wish it was something conventional like English Literature. Ugh! I hate the idea of putting some long dead writer under a microscope. Dammit, I'm proud to be a Physicist! I'll have my PhD. in the next couple of years."

"I'll bet that got Big Jim's attention."

"Did it ever," replied Marinda with slight giggle. "By the time we were done dancing I worked up the nerve to ask to see his laboratory."

"Dear, weren't you concerned that the Big Boy Scout would try to show you his etchings?" asked Delores with a perfectly straight face.

Marinda looked her directly in the eye. "If that had been the price for a tour of his lab, I'd have paid it. Willingly. I'm not the vestal scientist my parents seem to imagine." She blushed a bit before continuing, "At least not quite. But, he remained the perfect gentleman.

"I'm not trying to steal his work, but his opinions on what lines of research hold promise are invaluable to someone like me. He let me experiment with some of his electrical gear. Things I've only seen mentioned in the journals. And we talked theory. We even tore apart the science of some Buck Rogers style science-fiction gizmos. Most women, hell, most men too, would have been bored to death. To me it was refreshing. Exhilarating. Then we noticed that the sun was about to come up. We both got a little red faced.

"Before we left the lab I threw my arms around his neck and kissed him square on the mouth. I told him thank you for the wonderful evening, and night. He kissed me back. Really kissed me back. Whew! But he didn't try to advance. If he had, I'd have melted.

"Instead, he drove me home. Walked me to my parents' brownstone door and thanked me for a great time. I put my key in the door, but I tried to show him that I wouldn't mind another kiss. I think he started to grant my wish when all hell broke loose."

Jim Anthony regretted that his time with Marinda Stubbing was ending. At the same time he realized she was not for him. One of the reasons he dated was to take his mind completely off of his work, both as a scientist and what the papers had recently begun referring to as an adventurer. Still, one more kiss couldn't hurt. He leaned toward her slightly upturned lips when a huge crash reverberated through the heavy oak door of the luxurious brownstone.

"Marinda, stay behind me," Jim whispered as he swept her hand from the key. He turned it as quietly as possible. With the door open a few inches he looked inside. A man in the livery of an English butler lay sprawled in the remains of a heavy glass display case. His hand clutched a stout walking stick like a weapon.

Behind him he heard the girl whisper, "Gainor, oh no!"

Then Jim Anthony made a mistake. He figured he had delivered Marinda home just as a burglary went bad. The butler had been no match for one or two panicked crooks who even now probably were headed out the back door as fast as their legs could carry them. Jim opened the door to help the butler and to clobber any second story man dumb enough to hang around.

As he took in the scene in the foyer and beyond, his first muttered words in Comanche involving buffalo chips. Two heavyset men wearing identical suits topped with dark purple hoods faced the door in the vestibule. Two more stood in the room beyond. Another paused on the way up the stairs while yet two more popped out of a door under those same stairs.

Each hooded man seemed identical to the others except the one on the stairs. His hood sported a small orange flame painted on the forehead. The man looked at Jim Anthony, then behind him. "That's the girl," he called out. "Get her!"

Marinda knew a couple members of the Yale Boxing Team. She'd seen them train and fight. What seemed lightning fast to her before became turtle slow as she watched her date go into action.

Jim Anthony took one step into a flying side kick. The nearest hooded man stood about six feet tall. The pointed heel of Jim's shoe impacted next to his ear. As the man toppled, Jim rebounded from his hands in a forward flip into the second man in the vestibule. He augmented the impact with a hard driven leading elbow to the solar plexus. The man folded over on to him.

In the next split second Jim's fast moving hands frisked the mystery man. He removed a weapon of an unfamiliar feel, a wallet, and a strange apparatus from a holster opposite the gun. Then Jim heaved.

The heavyset man went flying. One of the men in the next room barely danced out of the way. His partner caught the heavy body full in the chest. He staggered backwards until a footstool tripped him. His head whacked the door post as he fell.

The "dancer" tried to get another of the strange weapons clear of its leather. Jim, his hands still full of pilfered gear, took two steps forward before diving enthusiastically into the infamous Ty Cobb sliding groin kick.

A quick glance behind assured him that Marinda was out of the line of fire of the other hooded men. Then Jim sprang to his feet without use of his hands. He leaped to the stairs, then up the seven steps to the slightly stunned leader of the group. Dropping the strange pistol he ripped the hood off of the man before he could react. The face seemed vaguely familiar, but he had no time for conjecture. The fellow yelled, "Gas it!" as he just managed to leap past Jim to the bottom of the stairs.

Instantly Jim heard several loud pops from the first floor. A split second later small capsules shattered in the vestibule area. A purple mist billowed throughout the front area of the floor.

Still in clear air, Jim filled his lungs to capacity. Then he glanced at what he still held in his hands. The wallet he reflexively put in a pocket. Then he peeled off the wrapper of the device from the second shoulder holster. He found he held a compact breathing device that had both a filter canister and small oxygen capsule. In an instant he clipped his nose closed and clamped his jaw onto the mouthpiece. A quick glance at the hood showed that it contained eye lenses. With the hood on, Jim headed down the stairs.

Keeping low, Jim looked around the banister. He saw a man holding his crotch shuffle through a door to the rear. The unconscious ones still lay where they fell. Jim raced back to the vestibule. The butler had no pulse. Not surprising, considering the stiletto driven in next to his sternum.

By the door Jim found Marinda coughing amid the thick purple fumes. As he dragged her outside she lost consciousness.

"Hold it right there, Mister Masked Man," came a sharp edged voice. Jim found himself looking down the barrel of a police service revolver.

"There's radio cars on the way from the precinct. Don't try nothing funny. There be good folks in these houses. We take alarms serious."

Very carefully Jim Anthony pulled off the purple hood. He took a full breath before spitting the breathing device into his hand.

"Officer, I'm Jim Anthony of The Daily Star. This is the daughter of the house. There's poison gas coming out that door."

The cop quickly backed down the steps to the sidewalk. Then he growled, "Bring her down easy! Let me get a look at you in the sunlight. I see anything funny in your hands and I shoot."

Jim moved as fast as he dared. He could feel that Marinda was barely breathing. He blinked as the sunlight hit him.

"I'll be darned. You are Jim Anthony, even if your hands and neck are all purple," exclaimed the cop. "What can I do to help?"

"Call for an ambulance with oxygen aboard. Then get the Fire Department on the way with gas masks," replied Jim.

"There be a call box on the corner," said the cop over his shoulder as he sprinted off.

A few minutes later Jim led firefighters inside to check for victims. He used clean mason jars from the kitchen to take air samples. He retrieved the weapon he had dropped on the stairs. Then he tried to draw the gas gun from the holster of one of the now very dead hooded men. Fortunately he noticed some wires running from the bottom of the holster to the man's belt. Jim hooked the grip of the weapon with a long piece of cord. When he pulled on the cord the gas gun exploded releasing another dangerous purple cloud.

By ten o'clock, Jim Anthony consulted with several doctors at the hospital on Roosevelt Island about Marinda's condition.

"We all agree," summed up Jim, "the gas acts as a blood poison, blocking oxygen absorption. Administering pure oxygen can stave off death in those with a medium exposure. Blood transfusions are the likely cure unless there is some other toxic component to the gas of which we are not yet aware.

"Thank you all very much for your quick work. The Police have not yet been able to locate Mr. and Mrs. Stubbing. However, it is a matter of public record that they left her in my care yesterday evening. Unless anyone has a legal objection I will continue to act as her guardian until she is able to say otherwise."

Henry Doric, the Captain of the local police precinct chuckled under his breath as he heard that. A moment later he joined Jim in an empty office.

"Well, Mr. Anthony," he said with a sly wink, "you sure staked your claim to responsibility for the young lady."

With a grim smile Jim replied, "Fortunately her mother's purchase got reported in all the society columns and our picture appeared in a couple of this morning's papers. Anybody, maiden aunt or family trustee, who wants to take her out of my care can go through my lawyers. After the message I left with the senior partner, that will take a minimum of six weeks.

"Miss Stubbing clearly was the target of those purple hooded killers. I'm sure you've heard from the downtown precinct that there were signs of a break in at the apartment she stayed in night before last. If I'd taken her home at any so-called reasonable hour she would be kidnapped or dead now. Your men, so far, have turned up no information about other incidents involving this group. I'm going to start certain 'special' sources digging into this matter. In the meantime, I want to quietly get Marinda transferred to the Waldorf-Anthony penthouse."

"I agree that she will be safer there," frowned the Captain, "but what about the guests and hotel staff?"

"I'll be taking a serious chance moving her even that far," replied Jim. "I can make the hotel safer than this hospital would ever be to a gas attack. I'll have the top four floors cleared out. Because of the experimental work that I sometimes do, the penthouse has an air handling system that should render that purple gas totally ineffective. Captain, your men, and the firemen, have worked wonders containing this deadly mess so far. Your detectives are digging like crazy for more information. If you can find a way to keep me informed, I'd appreciate it. I'm going to find these Purple Hoods. And believe me, they won't be happy about it."

———————————————————————————————

Frank Havens strolled up the street to the Clarion Building after having lunch at a quiet hole-in-the-wall beanery. He hummed the tune to a popular song as he walked. He returned greetings from the shop keepers, street vendors, and private citizens he passed. Everybody on these streets knew the crusading publisher of the Clarion newspaper chain.

One fellow stepped away from a newsstand holding a copy of the latest issue of Doc Savage. "Say, Mr. Havens. You're a coin collector. Take a look at what I got in change today!"

Havens deftly caught the tossed coin. An Indian Head penny dated 1907. Nothing all that special. Then he flipped it over. Another Indian, this one dated 1908. Havens blinked. "Now this is unusual! Care to sell it?"

"Be glad to," replied the roughly dressed man.

"Come on with me," said Havens cheerfully. "I'll have to make a call or two, to find out what it's worth."

A few minutes later, in Frank Havens office, Jim Anthony pulled off his shaggy brown wig and stretched to his full height. "That worked well," he observed, "but with the enemies you have, aren't you taking a chance bringing someone in off the street like that?"

"James, my boy," chuckled Havens, "for a block in all directions the streets are rigged in my favor. The fellow who sold you the magazine spent years in the Marines with Chesty Puller. Got almost as many medals. You'd shown any hostility to me, you would be in one tough scrap. Even with your skills. And he's not the only one in that area who either works for me, or owes me favors.

"You are about the last person I expected to see today. The Clarion graciously used up its own ink to put our rival's publisher in our society section. I figured you'd be sleeping off your big night on the town."

"I wish, Frank," said Jim with a sigh. "You heard about that brownstone gas leak?"

"Sure did," replied Havens. "Couple of fatalities and a whole block evacuated."

"Then the police have managed to keep the lid on," said Jim with a grim smile as he pulled two purple hoods, the gas gun and the breathing device from his baggy pockets. "The event happened at the Stubbing home, not the empty one two doors down as reported. Hooded marauders targeted Marinda Stubbing for either kidnapping or murder. I pulled this hood off the leader, but he got away. Let me borrow that pad of newsprint. Have you got an HB pencil?"

Soon a Clarion photographer shot Jim's highly detailed drawing of the leader of the hooded attackers so that copies could be made. Havens promised a quiet search for the identity of the man with his sources, including the mysterious sleuth known as The Phantom.

Shortly after that Jim Anthony left the Clarion Building with a sheaf of photographs of his drawing. At almost the same instant three bonded messengers hurried inside to pick up various envelopes containing copies of Jim's artwork. These were not eager young men in uniforms. They looked like the average fellow on the street. Except, that each carried a fully licensed automatic pistol that they knew how to use. Soon one began to make the rounds of the city's Federal Offices. Another spread copies to the N.Y.P.D. The third headed to Fort Dix in New Jersey.

Using the subway, and sometimes a taxi, Jim Anthony bounced around New York City for the next couple of hours. One day he planned to have an information network that spanned the entire metropolis. But in 1937 this was far from the case. He relied more heavily than he liked on Frank Havens, and a few others. Still he had some sources of his own. Before heading back to the Waldorf-Anthony he worked them diligently.

Soon his two headed Indian penny admitted him to the owner's quarters behind a small newsstand and cigar store in a slightly run down area. The proprietor knew nothing of the Purple Hoods or their equipment. But he blinked rapidly when he saw the likeness of the group's leader.

"Lord, he looks familiar. Must have been quite awhile. Not a crook... No, not a crook. Not a hanger on. Must be back while I was still a cop. Not a cop, either. Not even state police. Well, maybe, sort of related. Fed? Not FBI. Not Volstead related. What's left? What's left? State Department? No. War Department? That's it!

Intelligence. Army? No. don't think so... Navy... That's it. Naval Intelligence. Name. Name. Name. Something to do with heating. Stove, furnace, duct work, got it! Vents. Ventway? Venter, no. Vent-nor! That's it. I worked a case involving a waterfront dive pumping Navy men for information in '33. Harmon Ventnor worked the Navy side of the case. Smart man, but I always felt he'd be damn dangerous to cross."

One of the phone lines rang in the newspaper morgue of The Daily Star. The Crypt Keeper, as Robb Roberts sometimes called himself, took the lineman's handset off of his belt and plugged it into a nearby wall jack.

"Morgue. All the news that's fit to bury."

"Very funny, Robb," came Jim Anthony's voice sounding unamused. Robb heard traffic sounds in the background. "I need information on Harmon Ventnor of Naval Intelligence. Where he is. What he might be doing."

"He's dead, Jim," said Robb matter of factly. "Been dead for a couple of months according to the War Department."

"Then how did I happen to see him today?" asked a perplexed Jim Anthony.

"I'll look up the original citation, but I think facts were awful slim. Line of duty. Confidential assignment. That sort of thing. Course you know a lot more about impersonating the dead than most people, boss."

"You're right about that, Robb. Dump what you find to both the special teletype circuit and to the recorder at my penthouse. Second, add any hint of what he was working on. Third, find anything about thugs in business suits wearing purple hoods. Also, dig up the background on Robert Stubbing and his wife, Alicia Fortier Stubbing, and his business. Pay special attention to any possible connection to chemical warfare."

"Will do, boss," replied Robb. As soon as the connection ended he headed back into the files on his latest quest.

As he neared the Waldorf-Anthony Hotel, Jim planned to use the delivery entrance as he still wore the shaggy wigged disguise.

That was before he saw two newspaper reporters watching that door. As he circled the block he found other members of the fourth estate encamped. A glance into the lobby showed the Bell Captain jawing with Rex Parker, the bright young reporter of the New York Comet.

A few minutes later Jim Anthony used a tunnel to enter the sub-basement of the hotel. From there he made his way to the base of the shaft of his recently installed private elevator. To his surprise the car was aloft. Quickly he uncovered a hidden panel. The embedded counter showed only one movement that he could not account for. He glanced at the last bit of ticker tape that recorded the codes of the buttons pushed to activate service. Delores. Probably wanted a post date briefing.

Jim smiled. Smart, adventurous, and intensely loyal to her friends, the beautiful girl, no the beautiful woman Jim corrected himself, seemed just what he wanted in life. But should not have. His growing list of enemies would surely target her. Still, Jim felt himself longing for her touch as he climbed quickly up the elevator shaft.

At about the same time three heavyset men with overnight bags checked into the Waldorf-Anthony one after another. The desk clerk would later remember that the three had the same body type, but each had a different style of dress; spiffy, conservative, and threadbare. As the second of the three signed the register, a limousine pulled up to the front door. Out stepped a man in continental evening dress. His liveried private secretary and valet registered him as Sir Halley Gideon. Sir Halley took the large twentieth floor suite reserved for him by cable from his arriving ocean liner. Sir Halley's man asked that he not be disturbed as the crossing had been a rough one. Hardly had the well tipped bellman cleared the floor when the three heavyset men began to arrive unseen.

Just after the third man slipped in, a door at the other end of the floor opened. Another recently arrived guest soon asked the floor attendant for help with a possible bathroom fixture problem. The attendant easily solved the problem and returned to her desk shortly. In the short time she had been gone the five men from Sir Halley's suite summoned the elevator. As the door opened, the operator barely saw the incoming fist that put him in dreamland.

In the tiny hidden room that held the elevator entrance, Jim checked a board of lights and gadgets. All seemed well. He slipped into the penthouse proper.

As he passed the door of his personal suite he realized that he had donned his disheveled tuxedo about twenty hours previously. With that thought came the sudden feeling that his closed collar with bow tie felt like a noose. Jim didn't really like ties, at all. Yet his severely wilted black tie was more or less in place. Suddenly clothing flew in all directions.

Less than a minute later, clad only in a golden swimsuit with Comanche trim at the top, a more relaxed Jim Anthony entered his laboratory. He headed for the screen that allowed Marinda Stubbing some privacy in the very large open room. As he approached he heard the voice of the nurse.

"...have to leave soon. Miss Stubbing needs to rest as much as possible."

"If that's really necessary," came Delores' voice, "I'll wait for the Big Boy Scout in the parlor."

"I don't feel sleepy," said Marinda. "Not really, but I can tell I'm still dopey from whatever is going into my arms. Normally I'd ask for some of those scientific journals on that table. But right now I'm sure they'd read like Sanskrit. Maybe in a couple of... Oh,my! Either I'm hallucinating, or there's a bronze statue walking this way."

Delores turned, then chuckled. "No, dear. Your vision is 20/20. And that statue can be soft and cuddly, when he feels like it. Hello Big Jim. I've just been hearing how this gadget infested tennis court works as an aphrodisiac."

Jim Anthony actually blushed. His approach ended abruptly as he fumbled for words. "Why whatever do you mean, Delores?"

Delores pounced. Jim Anthony at a loss for words, amazing! "You Comanche Casanova! You brought this impressionable young scientist up to this hot bed of the latest discoveries. That's like making a just-into-port sailor the only judge for the Miss America pageant." Then she added with a smile and a wink, "You should be ashamed of yourself."

Not seeing the wink, Marinda felt shocked for a moment as Delores stalked over to the much taller man. Finally she managed to begin, "But Delores, he didn't..."

Delores hopped up to lock her arms around Jim's neck. In his ear she whispered, "Thanks for showing her such a good time, Mr. Gentleman Jim. I really like her. But, I still want you all for myself."

Marinda then watched Delores kiss Jim. The big man hesitated a moment then returned the kiss with a great intensity. She sighed to herself as she thought, "Me, put myself between those two again. No chance."

At the same time the purloined elevator arrived at the top of its normal run. Knowledgeable hands shifted a safety stop out of the way to allow the car to rise a short distance further. Now clad in dark coveralls, the five men formed a pyramid to let one of their number examine the emergency door to the top of the car. A moment later swearing drifted down.

"The flaming thing's got an alarm. Hand me the Yankee drill."

The leader glanced at his wrist watch.

A few moments later the nurse stood glaring at Jim, Delores, and Marinda with her pocket watch in her hand. In five more minutes she would throw the visitors out.

Suddenly Marinda's eyes widened. What little color there was drained from her face.

"Marinda, what is it?" asked Jim, his voice full of concern.

"I said I felt dopey. I didn't realize just how dopey. How could I forget? How could I? How is Gainor?" When Jim hesitated she gasped, "No. No. No! Is he..."

"I'm sorry, Marinda," replied Jim. "He was dead before the gas got to him. He was probably dead when he crashed into that cabinet."

Marinda did not speak. Did not move. Somehow her face slowly seemed to become devoid everything but the bone and cartilage below her skin. Delores told herself it was as if the other girl's soul imploded. Then tears began to flow from her eyes. She did not sob or cry. In fact she barely seemed to breathe. Soon Jim and the nurse each grabbed a hand to check her pulse.

The tears continued, but Marinda's heartbeat kept steady. Then a bit of color began to return to her face. Next her respiration became deeper. Finally, in a voice just above a whisper she moaned, "Oh Gainor. Gainor. What will I do without you?" Then she fell silent.

When she did not speak again, Jim asked, "Marinda, I'm sorry you had to find out this way. I take it that Gainor was with your family for a long time."

Marinda tried to blinked the tears away. "For as long as I can remember. Gainor was my anchor. My bedrock. He helped me understand the world beyond the circles my parents move in. My mother grew up in a remote part of provincial Canada. Now, she's is so in love with the idea of being in Society, with a capital 'S.' My father's business takes him all over. My mother sometimes goes with him, or travels with the 'in-season' crowd. The only thing that kept me from an English style boarding school was that Mama had a horrible experience with the one she got put in. So a lot of time I was home with just a string of governesses and Gainor.

"I attended about the most expensive private school in the area. A bunch of the brats there looked down on me because my father actually runs a company, instead of just clipping coupons like a brainless lounge lizard. Gainor helped me learn to

"You should be ashamed of yourself."

control my temper. My parents never realized how close I came to getting thrown out of school for returning insults with a swift kick, or three. He knew people in service all over the city. He started feeding me the dirt on the families of the kids who tried to make me miserable. Well, not adult dirt, but stuff nobody'd want bandied around.

"Anyway, I got a black eye in front of the whole Administration one day for mentioning that little Katherine's family fortune began when her great-grandfather beat a rap for horse thievery. While they dealt with Katherine and her toadies, they stuck me in the back of a tenth grade science class. I think they expected me to ignore the class and consider the problem I'd caused. If that was the idea, it sure backfired. I was fascinated while the teacher explained how electricity worked in lights, and motors, and the radio.

"When Gainor drove me home I kept asking him if he knew how this thing and that thing worked. I can still remember how he shut off my babbling. He told me, 'My dear young Marinda, yes, I know how those things work. If you wish, I can show you how make such devices yourself. Now you must keep this just between ourselves. And you must stay out of further trouble at school. I think we will start with a crystal radio set. You can listen to the voices of the air on an instrument you yourself built.' That was how I got started in science."

Jim nodded, "Obviously Gainor was a very wise man. I'm curious. Did he have a large amount of formal education?"

Marinda managed a small laugh, "Beyond the Three R's Gainor was completely self-taught. Under a couple of pen-names he wrote articles and do-it-yourself projects first for The Electrical Experimenter, then both Pop Mechanix, & Pop Science.

"My thesis adviser at Vassar is Dr. Grace Hopper. Her Doctorate in Electricity and Physics comes from Yale. One day when Gainor couldn't find me at my dorm room, he tracked me down to the Electrical Lab. While I finished up he quietly pointed out an error in the equations describing the function of a complicated circuit diagram on a blackboard. I cooled my heels for a solid twenty minutes while first Billings, the Graduate Assistant, then Dr. Hopper tried to prove him wrong. They couldn't."

Jim's eyebrows went up. He started to ask another question when the nurse intervened.

"Mr. Anthony, I must insist. Miss Stubbing needs to rest. Even more now that you've upset her. Everyone please leave now."

Finally the five gained the roof of the elevator car. Only to find heavy welded wire partitions blocking their access to other areas of the elevator and utilities control floor. The leader looked at his watch again. Their confederate arrived to lightly tap a code on the elevator door. Soon he began randomly running the car to various floors, but never opening the door. Wary of alarms the five attacked the barricades.

With Delores by his side Jim sought out Dawkins, his Cockney manservant. In the past Dawkins' duties appeared covered by the title, Valet, but nowadays Butler seemed to fit better. However, they located the little man in the penthouse kitchen.

The percolator pinged its way toward strong coffee. Three burners on the stove held covered pots. Jim's experimental electrical fruit juicer sat in the sink awaiting scrubbing. Shavings of two different cold cuts fell into the tray of the electric slicer while Dawkins seemed to be preparing a tossed salad. Delores and Jim stopped just inside the door. Without a word they turned to each other in wide eyed amazement.

Finally Jim Anthony managed to ask, "Dawkins, what is all this?"

The little Englishman turned around with a large carrot in one hand and a French knife in the other. Seeing his employer clad only in a bathing suit didn't even register as unusual any more to him.

"Good evening, sir. Miss Delores. Just preparing your castle for tonight's siege, sir."

Jim fought to keep his mouth from dropping open, "Siege, Dawkins?"

"Don't know what else to call it, sir. As far as the public's concerned, you've pulled up the drawbridge and cut yourself off from the outside world. The bars on the doors would take a perishing battering ram and fifty angry Celts to get through. We are hosting a very sick young woman who is supposed to start eating come morning. 'hi 'ave beef and bison stock simmering, and a thin porridge soaking over night. I can't order food sent up, so 'hi am preparing siege rations for them's got to stay the night. And, if I may say, sir, if I know you, you have hardly had a bite to eat or drink since that China chop house you took Miss Stubbing to last night. Please go seat yourselves in the dinning room. I shall serve in three minutes."

A moment later Jim passed Delores a steaming hot towel from the insulated caddy they found at the dining room table. Delores's chuckle almost became a giggle, "Well, I guess he told us..."

"He sure did," smiled Jim, "and he's right. I've been steadfastly ignoring my stomach's S.O.S. messages for hours. Dawkins knows me all too well."

Shortly Dawkins bustled in with a serving cart. "Here we are, Miss Delores, that Westphalian ham that you like so much, on whole wheat. And, for you sir, the bison salami that your cousin makes, on very dense Pumpernickel. The salad has the Mediterranean dressing of crushed garlic and dried mint in freshly extracted lemon juice and olive oil. Coffee will be ready shortly. It will be as strong as what both our Navies call 'mid-watch.' I do not recommend it if you plan to sleep in the near future. I shall have more food available for your selves, the nurse, and any allied forces, should they arrive."

As the little man finished unloading the cart, Jim asked, "Dawkins, I believe you belong to a social club or two for His Majesty's subjects who work on this side of the Atlantic."

Dawkins dropped his 'narration voice' at the question. "Indeed, I do, sir."

"And that means you are acquainted with many folks in situations similar to yourself, and that you hear stories about even more people. Am I correct?"

"Indeed, sir. However, it is not considered proper to repeat anything that 'appens at these places."

"I realize that, Dawkins. However, the man I need to ask about was murdered this morning. I gather, if ever someone deserved the term 'old family retainer,' Gainor, the Stubbing household's only live-in employee, was such a man. He died defending himself and the household. Can you tell me anything about him, including gossip."

Dawkins paused for a moment. Delores saw a series of expressions progress fleetingly across his face. Finally the little man tightened his jaw and spoke, "This Gainor chap did belong to one of the clubs, sir. I can't rightly remember ever meeting him. Perhaps I saw him a time or two, but I can't be sure. He was the subject of a lot o' talk, but not in a bad way. Very smart, they said. And supposedly very successful with the ladies in service. As you might think, that sort of thing can cause big trouble. But, they said that Gainor never courted others in the family's employ. Or even the staff of the h'mediate neighbors. Never a ripple of trouble. Hi can't say how much o' the stories 'appened, but most repeated the stories with respect for the man. And, a bit of envy. If you know what I mean, sir."

"Thank you Dawkins," replied Jim. "I want to catch the purple hooded gangsters who killed Gainor. You know I prefer not to pry into your private life. However, if you could somehow find out who were his most recent lady friends. If anything unusual happened in the Stubbing's neighborhood Gainor might have mentioned it to his lady friend. It's a long shot, but I hope you can help. Use the bootleg phone for any calls you make."

"Thank you for the confidence, sir. I shall make a call or two before the hour gets too late."

As Jim finished eating he told Delores, "I tried calling Tom earlier. I couldn't raise him at any of his usual haunts. If he doesn't call in soon I'll try the radio. Now, if you'd help me examine some evidence from the attack..."

"I'll help," replied Delores very sweetly. "But it's going to cost you."

Seeing the look on her face, Jim Anthony realized she wanted to rib him about something. It didn't take a genius to guess the subject. "Cost me what?" he said.

"Marinda told me she kissed you right on the mouth. And that you 'really' kissed her back. You are going to recreate that moment with me in her place. Then we'll see who's the better kisser!"

After several minutes of osculation Jim and Delores entered the small radio and recording studio in the penthouse. Jim carried an object in a heavy wax sealed container and a gas mask. As he opened the door of the broadcast room he briefed the girl.

"This contains the wallet I took off the living Purple Hood. The purple gas blanked or bleached everything of interest in the wallets the dead crooks carried. I had the thing X-rayed at the hospital. Nothing metal, or mechanical inside. I want to see if any information survived in this one. When I close this door you keep a sharp watch. If you see me act funny or see a hint of purple gas, throw the blower on full."

Intently studying the papers in the wallet Jim got yanked back to the here and now as Delores called out, "Jim, some lights just started flashing on the control panel."

Jim's head snapped up. Muttering to himself for concentrating too hard, he now noticed that the special attention light flashed in the small on-air room, as well. Quickly he spread the New York City phone book over the scattered papers from the wallet. As he exited the room he tripped the hidden blower switch. The upper pages of the phone book began to flutter.

A glance at the small block of lights unrelated to audio production and Jim hurried to the penthouse foyer with Delores trailing along.

"The private elevator's moving," said Jim as they entered. "Unfortunately, the television camera in the car takes about twenty minutes to warm up. Now let's see..."

Jim tripped a couple of hidden latches holding a near-perfect copy of Picasso's "Nude On A Black Armchair" to the wall hiding the secret elevator lobby. As he set the painting aside all the room lights automatically went off. Through a six inch thick set of tempered glass plates Jim and Delores could see clearly into the secret room. Jim held a lever in each hand. With them he could release tear gas, or fire fighting foam, or even electrify the carpet.

Then the two relaxed as Tom Gentry followed the elderly, but spry, Mephito from the cage.

"Tom looks tired," remarked Delores.

"And my grandfather looks concerned about something," said Jim.

"I'm glad you can read him," replied Delores ruefully. "I rarely can. Now I'd better go tell Marinda and the nurse about the new friendly faces. Poor Marinda sure doesn't need any more surprises today."

As Delores departed Jim replaced the painting just before Mephito emerged from the coat closet into the penthouse proper. Jim smiled and greeted him formally in Comanche, "Welcome, grandfather."

The old man's expression did not change. "Thank you, grandson. Please join me at the place-of-fire." With that the Shaman departed.

Jim shook his head slightly. Turning to Tom he asked, "What in the world is going on?"

"He called me from the Teepee to pick him up," began Tom. "You know how much he hates using the phone. But he must have called half a dozen places before he caught me at McGinty's Lunch Counter by the airport. Something's really getting under his skin. He seemed impatient while I refueled the plane to come back. And I darned near put on the pilot's oxygen mask 'cause he kept lighting his medicine sticks every time we hit a bump coming back. All the years I've known him, don't think I've ever seen him wound so tight."

"Thanks, Tom," said Jim. "I agree. Something's got his attention. Delores'll fill you in on what's happened to me in the last twenty-four hours." With that Jim Anthony headed for the place-of-fire, meaning the large fireplace in the parlor.

Jim was not surprised to find Mephito sitting on the brick skirt next to the just lit fireplace. As he entered he watched his grandfather sprinkle a powder from his medicine bag over his fire sticks. Then the old man snatched a bit of kindling out of the fire and dropped it onto the carefully arranged sticks. With a small flash a pungent, but pleasant smelling smoke billowed up. The draft of the flue sucked most of it up the chimney, but enough remained that Jim could smell it as he folded his tall frame to sit "Indian style" across from Mephito.

Memories paraded through Jim's mind from his entire life. Memories about the wonders of nature and the history and customs of the Comanche people Mephito taught him as they sat by various kinds of fire. He waited quietly.

Finally, in Comanche, the old man began, "Grandson. The spirits awoke me just before dawn. In the smoke and fire of the sticks I saw you with a woman of much learning. And then a strange smoke covered you both. That smoke was of the color the Europeans call 'Royal.' The vision faded. When I lit the sticks again I did not see you. I believed that you were safe, at least then. But a single spirit called out to me. That spirit feared for you, and the woman. The spirit foretold of more danger when the two of you were together. Again the vision faded. I have reached out to the spirit again. Many times, but he has been silent. Now the sticks foretell the Royal smoke will come again. I go now to prepare." With that, Mephito placed the fire sticks into his medicine pouch. He rose and left the room.

Jim Anthony sat unmoving as he digested his grandfather's latest revelation from the spirits. Far too many of these visions came true in some form for Jim not to take Mephito seriously. A moment later he rose.

Before he took three steps Dawkins' voice came over the intercom, "Mr. Anthony. The hotel manager is on the house phone. 'e says hit might be important." Jim snatched up the nearest instrument.

"Mr. Anthony," said the on-duty manager of the Waldorf-Anthony, "one of the elevator operators has disappeared. A bellhop noticed that an elevator seemed stalled on five. The front desk called the floor attendant. She said that the door had not opened at all. Maintenance found the car parked about two feet above the fifth floor level. Nobody was aboard. We are searching for the operator."

"Thank you for keeping me informed," said Jim. "Please try to determine if the door to the roof of the car has been opened."

"Will do, Mr. Anthony."

"Problems, Jim?" asked Tom from the room's door. Jim turned around to find that his best friend had shucked his preferred aviator clothing for a conservative business suit. A business suit expertly tailored to conceal a shoulder holster and some other things.

"Probably, old friend," began Jim. "There's an elevator operator missing in the hotel. That may mean that bad guys are on this level, or above. And, Mephito believes that damn purple gas will show up again. You know where the gas and oxygen masks are. Please see that all seven people in the penthouse have them, and know how to use them. I'm going to take a few precautions."

As Jim hurried to the floor's utility closet he glanced into the room devoted to Indian artifacts. Along with the headdresses, pottery, and clothing, the room contained many examples of weapons from all over the Americas. Jim was not surprised to see most of the weapons missing from their places. Only an expert would realize that those spears, clubs, knives, bows and arrows, not to mention the many tomahawks, were modern reproductions, fully ready for battle. If not finished now, Mephito would soon completely seed every room with something both he and his grandson knew how to use to deadly effect. Jim smiled grimly. By now the old man probably carried his beloved Winchester '73 rifle and a few surprises.

As Jim flipped switches and cross connected circuits, Mephito entered the large laboratory room. After slipping an Iroquois war club behind the water cooler, he walked silently over to where Tom and Delores were instructing the nurse and Marinda on the use of the gas masks.

Delores felt more than saw the slender old man arrive. She turned with a huge smile for the Shaman. In almost perfect Comanche she said, "Welcome, grandfather of the man I love."

"Thank you, daughter," Mephito replied in the same tongue. Then he switched to English after Delores introduced him. "Woman of learning, medicine woman and she-who-plays-with-lightning, must also be brave now. I ask the spirits to watch over you."

With that he placed the ceramic bowl of a mortar on the table next to the bed. In it he arranged his fire sticks. A moment later a small amount of smoke rose up from them. From inside his vest he produced a long feathered totem. He stepped to the hospital bed. He placed the strange device in Marinda's hands.

"Keep near you," he said. His body blocked the others from seeing as he showed Marinda the long sharp knife the totem concealed. Marinda placed the object in her lap.

Much muffled cursing went on above the laboratory. Very heavy padding covered the ventilation stacks. Padding held in place by seemingly countless electrified wires. An alarm net. The floor of the extremely short attic consisted of heavy chrome steel plates. What explosives they carried would hardly breach the plates at all. All air intakes seemed to be below, as well.

Above an unprotected corner room they rigged a charge to drop part of the ceiling. Timer ticking they hurried to other areas. Two of the men, now all in purple hoods, removed the louvers of an attic vent on the south side. Two more popped out of a small access door on the east side of the penthouse's decorative roof. The last man returned to the elevator shaft and exited to the highest piece of roof of the Waldorf-Anthony. Quietly he scampered to where the higher area overlapped the penthouse. All five waited for the explosion.

In the laboratory Delores felt, but did not hear, the explosion shake the penthouse. Neither she, the nurse, nor Marinda heard the crashing sound as the two teams of Purple Hoods smashed through the heavy windows into two widely separated sections of the penthouse.

Jim Anthony looked at the lights displayed on main panel of the penthouse's burgler alarm. The explosion in the corner room did not worry him. The room was a trap. The ceiling could easily be breached, but penetrating the walls, the floor, and the door, required enough explosive that any half sane attacker would know that he could not survive the blast. Before dashing out of the utility closet Jim spoke into a microphone of a unique radio that broadcast through the electrical wires of the structure. Tom, Mephito, and Delores wore tiny crystal sets tuned to the system. He gave the room numbers of the break-ins and assigned one room to the others.

As Jim finished speaking, the fifth man then began to jimmy the window to Dawkins' private room. Any slight noise he might make would go unnoticed amid the reaction to his colleagues' spectacular entrance. Jim silently headed out just before another light on the panel changed.

On the south side, the two Hoods scrambled to their feet in the parlor. With gas guns in one hand and Colt Model 1911's in the other they opened the door to the silent penthouse corridor. Suddenly the first man tried not to howl in pain. He dropped his automatic. His forearm seemed to be on fire. He tried to move the limb to where he could see it better. His arm would not move. Deep under his hood his eyes went wide. An arrow served to nail his arm to the door jamb. As he jerked his head back another arrow pinned his hood to the wood.

The other two invaders glanced briefly at the Indian artifacts in the room. They drew their weapons and headed for the room's two doors.

"This one's locked," whispered the man at the door to the corridor.

"This one isn't," replied his partner as he began to open the door to the next room.

He started to step through, but the door slammed shut as if his two hundred pounds were not in the way. Jim Anthony hit the door's edge with all the force he could put into a flying dropkick. Smashed in the face with his own gas gun, the Purple Hood sailed a good ten feet back into the room.

His bare feet silent, Jim dashed out of Mephito's bedroom. When he reached the door to the Indian room he slid back the silent hidden bolt keeping the portal closed. He flipped the door open, then slid through, losing some belly skin to the wood floor.

Back at the parlor Tom whispered to Mephito, "I've got 'em. See if there are any others."

The old man grunted, but Tom thought he heard the word "distraction" float back as the old Shaman vanished like a shadow.

Tom covered the door with his pistol. From a pocket he removed one of Jim Anthony's inventions. The transparent pouch contained two chemical compounds. Tom pulled a small lanyard that caused the two liquids to mix in the presence of a catalyst. Bubbles began to form. Almost instantly the bag became nearly as hard as a softball. He pitched it underhand into the doorway. By the time the pouch landed it coldly glowed like burning magnesium. Not to mention that the bubbling gas created forced open a valve to a piercing air whistle. Keeping low, Tom moved toward the door. He heard a cry of anguish as the pinned arm disappeared back into the room.

The leader of the Purple Hood team, so proclaimed by the flame drawn on his hood's forehead, hurried through the uncontested part of the penthouse. The floor plan fresh in his mind from the City's most up to date records, he carried an extendable titanium steel wrecking bar that, given his strength, should open any door this side of a vault. Every air vent he encountered roared with suction. He realized that the purple gas would be little more than an annoyance here. He passed some windows to the laboratory, but they were shuttered. Finally he reached the laboratory door with its thick, wire reinforced, window. Ducking down he inserted the pry bar into the door's frame next to the lock. After looking both ways down the corridor he threw all his strength onto the fully extended bar.

Delores heard the heavy Yale lock twist and snap just before the west door of the laboratory slammed open. Whirling, she saw a man in a purple hood scramble upright as he drew a heavy automatic pistol. She snapped off a shot with the .32 automatic she carried. The bullet smashed into the metal door frame just behind the charging man.

Jim Anthony took in the situation as he slid across the Indian room floor. One Purple Hood lay crumpled against the base of a display case. The other tried to reset himself after dodging the flying door. As the man tried to bring the gas gun to bear, Jim rolled toward him. A gas shell whizzed far over him to impact on the room's other door. Jim ended his roll face down. His body rigid from head to toe, his arms flat against his sides to the elbows, he raised himself up like a gymnast on the pommel horse.

Trying to bring his automatic around the Purple Hood saw muscles pop out all over his adversary's body. Too late he realized that he stood within range of those bare legs. Before he could begin to move back, Jim Anthony's whole body pivoted like a released spring. Jim's flying feet hooked the Purple Hood's legs completely out from under him. He landed skull first on the hard oak floor.

Over the noise of the ventilation system Tom Gentry heard a lamp crash to the floor in the parlor. Sounds of furniture moving followed. The bright light abated as something covered it. Then the anguished cries of pain ended abruptly. Automatic in firing position, Tom risked a dash across the doorway.

A shaft of the bright light outlined a Purple Hood climbing back out the window with a rope in his hands. Tom reversed field. As he dived through the door he fired rounds into the easy chair and couch that might hide the other attacker. He rolled to his feet. Nobody else remained in the room. Tom carefully looked out the window. Just in time to see a hooded man smash into the window of a room three stories below.

Still vigilant, Tom called the hotel security office. "There is an armed man loose on the thirty-first floor. Last seen wearing a dark suit and a purple hood. If seen shoot first, then ask questions. Got that? Also, when the police arrive tell them that there is the body of another Purple Hood on the twenty-sixth floor setback ledge."

Delores kept count of the rounds she fired at the fast moving Purple Hood. The weapon only contained seven. The man ran broken field through the maze of laboratory equipment like a college halfback. Her third round splanged off the roaring ventilation system surrounding a long chemical bench. Instinctively she aimed where the man should appear past the sheet metal enclosure. He did not.

Too late she realized he had doubled back. Her head turned faster than her arm could. She saw the Purple Hood point his .45 straight at her heart.

To her surprise she tried to swear, rather than scream, as the man's finger began to tighten. Then something spun into her frozen field of vision. The hooded man simply pitched forward. The pistol discharged harmlessly as it hit the floor.

Delores did cry out then. Just one word, "Grandfather!" For sticking out of the Purple Hood's upper spine was the half buried copper blade and handle of a tomahawk.

NYPD Inspector Gregg decided this would be a really long night. Gregg often worked closely with the master detective known as The Phantom. Lately some of his

"Jim's flying feet hooked the Purple Hood's legs..."

superiors seemed to have decided that he should take the call every time some high powered civilian tangled with weird characters. Captain Doric had filled him in on the morning's deadly fracas, with poison gas, no less.

Finally enough men had arrived so that he could hold the hotel perimeter and begin the room by room search to find the missing Purple Hood reported by Jim Anthony. Search underway, Gregg took the elevator to the penthouse.

As Gregg stepped into the foyer he heard the rush of air through the vents. Then an honest to gosh English butler offered to guide him. In the first room they passed Gregg saw a body on the floor, under a sheet. The sight of the second room caused his jaw to drop open a bit. Two men, looking like the losing end of a Pier Six brawl, were tied to stout but fancy wooden chairs. In front of them sat a wrinkled old man, ramrod straight, in highly decorated denim. He sat Indian fashion. Gregg thought he looked like a much thinner version of the Indian on the buffalo nickel. The old man held a lever action rifle like he knew how to use it.

Then the English guy told him, "This way into the la-bor-a-tory, sir."

A very brief time later Gregg realized that Jim Anthony's concise report left only a couple of his questions unanswered.

With those out of the way, Jim asked, "There is still no sign of Marinda's parents?"

"It's like they've fallen off the edge of the world," replied Gregg. "Stubbing often hears of some new discovery and rushes out to sign up the inventor. Sometimes his wife goes along. And all very hush-hush. I've got people checking on their cars and private plane."

"That would be one huge coincidence," said Jim with a wry smile. "You've seen my sketch, I take it? Good. Keep this under your hat, if you can. That sketch has been identified as an officially dead member of Naval Intelligence."

"You're serious?!"

"Yes, I am, Inspector. But you know from long experience that the face I saw might not be his real one. Is the FBI being helpful?"

"We're still waiting for word on the prints and pictures."

Just then Dawkins' voice again came over the intercom. "Mr. Anthony, a gentleman for you on the second outside line. Mr. Gleason is the fellow's name."

Dawkins use of the word "fellow" meant that Robb Roberts, Mr. Gleason, had given the day's code signaling that he was not under duress. He put the receiver to his ear with, "Jim Anthony."

"Can you talk, boss?" came Robb Roberts excited voice.

"I'm listening, Mr. Gleason."

"You have company, I see."

"That's right."

"Here's the dope. There's nothing in the files about those Purple Hoods. Probably shouldn't officially be anything, but some information did come in back last July. Happened when I was out in New Mexico visiting Dr. Goddard. One of our stringers reported some sort of raid on a company making echo-location equipment for ships and submarines. Happened in Connecticut. Some guys in purple hoods hit the place like Dillinger's gang on a bank heist. Supposedly carted off a pile of stuff.

The stringer no sooner finished talking to our stenographer than the Navy grabbed him. Less'en an hour later some Navy Captain rolled through the managing editor's office. Said the stringer stumbled into a training exercise. Asked that everything about the event be destroyed and forgotten. Gordon, my replacement, even turned in the onion skin copy sent to the morgue. When nothing showed up I checked with him. Been grilling him, but I doubt there'll be any real details. He never read the whole report. The stringer graduated college and went who knows where. And the steno's now Mrs. Somebody in Tulsa. That's about it, boss."

"Thank you, Mr. Gleason," said Jim. "Do you have any suggestions?"

"I could check with my opposite numbers at the Sentinel, and a couple of other places."

"You do that, Mr. Gleason," replied Jim as he hung up the phone.

Vassar Graduate Assistant in Science Ryan Billings glanced at his wristwatch. Five minutes ahead of schedule. Smiling, he stopped at an intersection near the Vassar campus. Carefully he placed the Thermos of hot coffee and the bag of donuts he carried on the ledge of a Post Office drop box. He pulled a donut out of the bag. Chewing on his first bite he retrieved the copy of Weird Tales from his coat pocket. Deftly he flipped the magazine open to his bookmark. Just enough time to get Jules De Grandin started on his newest case. He tilted the book to where the streetlight seemed brightest. As he began to read this new tale of the unexplained he did not notice the mysterious figure steal out of the alley behind him. Strong arms snatched him away like he was on rollers. Amazingly, the donut landed back on top of its bag. Weird Tales went straight up, then fell spine first to open at the bookmark again. Ryan took no notice.

"Depending on the week of the month," laughed Marinda during her date with Jim Anthony, "Ryan'll be carrying Amazing Stories, Astounding, Weird Tales, or Thrilling Wonder Stories with him. He'll stop to read at the same place until the absolute last second before he has to unlock the doors of the science building."

Ryan Billings could not move. He felt enclosed in a flesh and blood vise. Glancing around he realized he was in the recessed doorway to the butcher shop that fronted around the corner from where he had been standing. No one could see him from the street. Then came an authoritative voice in his ear.

"Ryan, I'm not going to hurt you. I need your help, but not in public. My name is Jim Anthony. Do you know of me?"

The rock like hand came off of Ryan's mouth. "The Jim Anthony who wrote the piece on better vacuum tubes in the Physics Journal?"

"Among other things," replied Jim. "I have identification, including my American Physics Society membership card. I need to secretly get on campus to talk with Dr. Hopper. I'll make that worth your while."

Suddenly released, Ryan watched as the tiniest flashlight he had ever seen illuminated first a series of identification cards, then the living face of the man pictured on some of them.

"Ryan, I'm sorry to have scared you, but my errand is really important. Will you help me?"

"Okay, Mr. Anthony, but it will cost you."

"How much?"

"Not money. That's too easy. You cracked that murder case at the donut factory where E.E. Smith works. Doc's got a new serial called 'Galactic Patrol' about to start in Astounding. I want autographed copies of all the issues."

Jim Anthony half strangled to keep from laughing out loud. "Done," he said with a smile.

Before Jim could begin to question the graduate assistant, he found himself grilled. "Mr. Anthony, does this involve the accident near Marinda Stubbing's home? The campus radio station picked up on that gas leak and that Marinda got hospitalized."

Score one for the Journalism Department, Jim told himself. "Ryan, I'm going to take a further chance on you. That was no accident. I believe you met her man Gainor. He was murdered. And Marinda was attacked by a group of purple hooded thugs. It's possible they wanted her as leverage against her father. But if she was the actual target I need to know why. Is Marinda involved in any sensitive research, especially that the War Department might be interested in?"

"No, sir. Anything like that would probably be above my level, let alone hers. She's been working on contained dynamic airflow with Professor Anderson. The only folks interested in stealing that research would be Bissell, Hoover, and Electrolux, for their vacuums."

Jim tried again. "Is there anyone, from outside the school, who regularly checks for new lines of research. Or asks about important discoveries?"

Ryan thought for a moment. "Regularly? Not really. A lot of visitors pay courtesy calls when they are on campus. Nobody... Well, except for that Navy character. I think he's connected to their R.O.T.C program. Drives and flies around the region. He comes by about once a month on his route. And of course Vassar doesn't have R.O.T.C. He stops at every branch of the Science Department. Commander Hershell's the name. And a real Jekyll and Hyde. One visit he smiles and tells a joke or two. The next he acts like I'm trying to pick his pocket. Come to think of it, he's due to come by today or tomorrow. Now we'd better get going, or I'll have to carry you in as a parcel."

Ryan slipped Jim into the basement of the main Science Building. Jim rode up alone three floors in a tiny freight elevator that threatened to come apart with each new bump it passed. Slightly out of breath, Ryan opened the door to the cage and rushed Jim into an office.

"Dr. Hopper'll be here in about twenty minutes," Ryan whispered. "I better tip her she has a visitor. She might try to brain you with her briefcase, otherwise."

Pointedly ignoring the large man who rose from her office visitor's chair as she entered, Dr. Grace Hopper, PhD, hung up her coat, placed a slim briefcase next to her typewriter, and settled her purse into a desk drawer. Only then did she acknowledge Jim Anthony's existence.

"Ryan Billings told me that I had a secret visitor that he would vouch for. I believe I recognize you. However, if this is any kind of a prank, stop it right now. With

Marinda Stubbing hospitalized, I see no reason for humor."

"Nor do I, Dr. Hopper," replied Jim. "I am Jim Anthony. Here are several credentials. And, I'm sure we could reach one or more mutual acquaintances by telephone, should that be necessary. I am here about Marinda Stubbing. She is recovering nicely. However what you have heard is neither the full or correct story of the incident. When I took her home after our evening together..."

Grace Hopper shook her head for a moment when Jim Anthony finished his recital. She stepped to a filing cabinet and removed a folder. After a glance at the contents she began, "Robert Stubbing began his career by patenting a major improvement in the facsimile transmission of pictures. After I first met Marinda I began to keep an eye out for his company's name in the journals and so forth. He has helped bring into use discoveries in almost every field of research. And often from totally obscure sources. When I became her adviser she sometimes showed me the huge differences between what her father first saw and the finished project. Making things practical is her father's gift. Recently Marinda showed me a fascinating work in progress. Do you recognize what these are?"

Jim took the sheaf of papers Dr. Hopper offered him. The flimsy yellow papers, torn off just longer that letter size paper, were covered with columns of figures. After a brief study he replied, "Arc-tangent tables to six decimal places. Sent over a teletype system, by the look of them."

"Yes, and no," said Dr. Hooper. "The teletype simply served to print the figures. A convenience. Tell me, Mr. Anthony, are you familiar with the work of Charles Babbage?"

"The creator of the so called Differential Engines? My father once took me to a demonstration at the London Science Museum. That was with the machine completed in 1891, twenty years after his death. Being very young I was more fascinated by watching all the beautiful moving and spinning parts than the numbers on the little windows. Thirty one decimal places of accuracy, as I recall."

"And you remember how big the machine was?"

"About eight feet tall. A sign said it weighed a couple dozen tons."

"Would you agree that Babbage's machine is still the state of the art in mechanical calculation?"

"Yes, I would, Dr. Hopper, barring some highly secret project."

"Those tables you are holding were calculated in less than ten minutes and fed to the campus radio station's teletype machine by a device about half the size of a shoe box simply plugged into the same electric circuit as the teletype."

Flabbergasted. That term rarely applied to Jim Anthony concerning the subject of science. Dr. Hopper did not recognize the language of the expression that came out of Jim's astonished mouth. Roughly translated: "May I fall down a prairie dog hole and be buried in buffalo chips."

"Astonishing isn't it, Mr. Anthony?"

"More than astonishing, Dr. Hopper. Revolutionary. An electrical calculating machine that small, and that fast... Can it do more than arc-tangents?"

"Marinda told me it would do all trigonometric functions, and various log functions with minor adjustments. But the thing was temperamental. The box is covered with tiny screwdriver adjustment slots, a couple dozen at least. Marinda tuned the machine with them using what looked like a miniature RCA Magic Eye display. She worked over twenty minutes to do it. When the run was over the box needed her attention again. As to accuracy, she showed me a special connector to link up to six units together. That accuracy would equal or outdo even Babbage."

Dozens of mathematical possibilities raced through Jim's mind. The number seemed to grow exponentially. Finally he shook his head to clear it.

"I went into a similar trance, Mr. Anthony. The possibilities seem endless."

Returning to his mission Jim asked, "Who knows about this?"

"Besides Marinda and myself, just Ryan. He arranged for the use of the teletype after the radio station was off the air for the evening."

"None of the station's staff saw what happened?"

"So far as I know, no. I signed for the use of the teletype and for the responsibility of locking up the facility."

"Dr. Hopper, does the radio station have any connection to the United States Navy?"

"The Navy? Why do you ask?"

"Because the Navy or people connected to the Navy keep popping up in relation to those Purple Hoods. I even understand that you get regular visits from their R.O.T.C representative. Given your student body, that seems a bit strange."

"While not as frequent, the Army also looks in on our science programs. Just a minute. The radio station's Chief Engineer. He's called Sailor Sparks by some of the students. He's a retired Navy signal man."

Waiting down the hall from Dr. Hopper's office, Ryan Billings flinched as he heard his name in the loudest tone she ever used. He hurried back to her door.

"Ryan," asked Dr. Hopper, "do you have any idea where Sailor Sparks could be found at this hour?"

"Let's see. He rooms at Dr. Zircon's home. He usually has breakfast at the Student Union. There's a decent chance he's there now."

"Thank you, Ryan. I must be in class in five minutes. Please help Mr. Anthony find that man. But if trouble should start you skedaddle. Understand?!"

"Yes, Ma'am! Come on, Mr. Anthony. The back stairs will be faster. And less visible."

Ryan took off at a run without looking to see if Jim followed. Jim gave Dr. Hopper brief thanks, then followed. By vaulting the railings of several flights of stairs he caught up with Ryan at the building door.

Jim kept the pace to a brisk walk as they crossed the campus. He did not want to draw any more attention than he had to. When they reached the building that housed the Student Union Ryan led him off the sidewalk to a window in the north side of the structure. The grass vanished under foot at that point. Ryan peeked into the window.

"From here I can see the facility dining area," said Ryan. "You always check here if you don't want to meet one of your professors. There he is. Looks like he's about done. Wait a sec... There's Commander Hershell walking up to his table!"

"Get me there," instructed Jim.

Ryan led Jim into the Faculty Only area of Union just a few seconds later. There was no sign of Sailor Sparks except for a spilled cup of coffee next to his plate. Then Jim caught a glimpse of part of a Navy uniform vanishing behind a closing door.

Jim paused just long enough to say, "If you see Sparks call Dr. Hopper. Otherwise, stay clear."

That said, Jim Anthony sprinted for that door like his shoelaces were on fire. As he ran he pulled four small spheres out of his suit pockets.

The door opened at the bottom of a little used stairwell. Jim ascended the first flight in two long steps. He heard the sound of a door closing above him. With two more huge strides he gained the door. Ducking low he went through. He heard a familiar popping sound. Something whizzed above his head to shatter on the wall of the stair landing. In a move almost too fast for the eye to follow Jim threw one of the spheres to the rear where it would impact almost on top of the purple gas shell. Simultaneously, Jim yanked the door closed. A faint woofing sound came through the door as Jim saw Commander Hershell chamber the second of the four rounds the gas gun held. He hurried forward.

A split second later two things happened. Compressed air hurled a new gas cannister faster than the best Major League arm could throw it. And Jim Anthony threw his second sphere at about the same velocity. The two projectiles smashed together about halfway between the men.

The emerging purple gas vanished in a cloud of white powder. Made largely of super-fine baking soda and some other chemicals, the powder neutralized the somewhat acidic gas.

By the time the white powder erupted Jim Anthony had wound up like that Major League pitcher. He arrowed his third sphere through the blinding white cloud straight to where Commander Hershell stood. Jim heard a yelp of surprise competing with the sphere's woof. Footsteps pounded a retreat as he closed his eyes to charge through the settling cloud.

By the time Jim reached the end of the corridor of Student Union offices and emerged into the crowded entryway Commander Hershell had vanished. In more ways than one.

He found the remains of a Navy uniform blouse draped over a pamphlet rack. The pants had been flung aside nearer the entrance. Outside the door Jim found Commander Hershell's face. Sort of.

Jim picked up the full face mask. A quick glance across the quadrangle showed only people who looked like they belonged. Nobody acted at all suspicious.

Jim stepped back into the Student Union. Puzzled students were looking at the discarded clothing. Jim looked, as well. Thin stitching, like a tailor's basting thread covered the inside of the garment. Ingenious, thought Jim, one outfit basted over another. Yank, Yank, and you wore a completely different outfit. One more yank and your face changed, too. Jim folded the face mask carefully into a large linen handkerchief. He headed back to Dr. Hopper's office to leave advice for cleaning up the Student Union.

Jim Anthony flew a well used looking rental plane back to New York City from the flying field near Vassar College. The trip took more time that he wanted, but the Thunderbird, his personal speedster, was far too well known. Well known to government officials, reporters, and to his enemies. He used the time to reflect on the case. Suddenly, it seemed that "Sailor Sparks" Murphy, former top Navy radio rating, could not be found at work, or in his lodgings. Murphy was last seen having breakfast at the Student Union at about the same time Commander Hershell had been seen entering the building. Now both could not be found. And if either the Purple Hoods, or the Navy itself, sought scientifically advanced devices, the potential of Marinda's mysterious half-shoe box calculating machine would shine in their eyes like a parachute flare. Marinda needed to tell him about the device.

Jim landed on a small Long Island field, reclaimed the common appearing car he'd arrived in, and headed for Manhattan. As soon as he arrived in the Waldorf-Anthony penthouse he knew something was wrong. The place seemed like barely organized bedlam. He could hear more than one raised voice. Tom, for one sounded upset. Someone with a Brooklyn accent seemed to be exchanging words with someone at a police precinct. Down the hall Inspector Gregg's hard edged voice asked pointed questions that received no answers.

Suddenly Jim realized Dawkins stood beside him. "What in the name of a Painted Puffet is going on, Dawkins?"

The little man swallowed, "H'im sorry to report, sir, that Miss Stubbing has vanished." Dawkins knew he never wanted to hear the translation of the Comanche words that then burst from his employer's lips.

"Sorry, Dawkins. Tell me what happened."

"Yes, sir. Per your instructions the Nurse Ames removed all the medical paraphernalia from Miss Stubbing's person as soon as she awoke. Miss Stubbing then ate the light breakfast I'd prepared with no ill effects. She then dressed, or so I'm told, in some of Miss Delores' clothing. The nurse and I then installed her in the number three guest room with the nurse in the connecting room, should she be needed. Hit's been determined that Miss Stubbing began to use the phone. Soon thereafter she apparently slipped into the elevator. The car was blocked from rising to the penthouse, but not from descending. She simply walked out of the hotel."

Not much later Jim Anthony took Tom Gentry with him to a bonded warehouse in which he was a silent partner. They shifted steamer trunks, packing cases, and portable desks until they found a crate marked "Turkey 1920-1921." The crate contained business records of Sean Boru Anthony, some knickknacks, many color photographs of the East, and three journals.

As Jim began to peruse the journals, Tom looked at the photos. Each one had a detailed explanation on the back. "Look for pictures of U.S. Navy vessels or personal," Jim told him. "Tell me the dates."

Tom flipped through the pictures more quickly. "What are we looking for?"

"Leverage."

At 5:47 that same day a Navy Staff Car pulled up to the large house outside

Washington, D.C., designated Number One Observatory Circle. The driver alighted and hurried to open the rear passenger door.

Out stepped Admiral William D. Leahy, Chief of Navel Operations. "Put the car away, Petty Officer Warren," said the Admiral wearily. "I hope to heaven I'm done for the day."

The driver saluted with a knowing nod and departed. The Old Man entered his official residence before the staff car left the block. Not five miles down the road the driver groaned. A motorcycle approached from the opposite direction. Astride the top of the line Indian machine sat a Marine Corps officer. There was no mistaking the Leatherneck's mission. An official dispatch case hugged the small of his back. The driver hesitated. Finally he shrugged to the world at large and headed back towards Observatory Circle.

The driver parked on the road behind the Admiral's quarters. Using the garden hedges for cover he slipped into the attached garage and climbed into the loft above. Under a blanket he peered through a tiny crack into the CNO's study.

CNO Leahy began to relax. The household staff held dinner pending his wife's return from a Navy League meeting. Shoes off, uniform blouse hanging up, the Admiral fixed himself a highball from the bar hidden in his study. He needed to unwind. He needed to laugh. The simple humor of the night's Charlie McCarthy radio program seemed just what he needed. If there were no interruptions. At that moment he heard a powerful motorcycle in the distance. A moment later the Chief Petty Officer on watch stuck his head into the study as he knocked, "Dispatch rider comin' in, sir!"

Soon a very striking Marine First Lieutenant entered and saluted. "Good evening, sir. I was instructed that the contents of the pouch are for your eyes only, but they are not to leave my sight."

Leahy waved the CPO out of the room. The Marine unlocked the case and approached. As the man came nearer the Old Man realized just how big the fellow really was. Over six feet with a build like a lantern-jawed Charles Atlas advertisement. Something seemed familiar about him. Leahy dismissed the thought. He met so many young men of all types that they seemed to blend together.

Quickly he opened the envelope the pouch contained. There were two items. First, a dated color photograph of a motor whaleboat pulling away from a pier. The uniformed passengers in the photo looked more than a little the worse for wear, but all smiled. Even the two on stretchers. Catching his breath the Admiral turned over the other piece of paper. An invoice, headed with Celtic decorative letters "S.B.A., Ltd." Below the heading, written with a C-3 Speedball pen, were the words: "Bill Due Now."

"What is the meaning of this?" gasped the Chief of Naval Operations.

Jim Anthony removed the cheek pads and over-dentures from his mouth saying, "That's what I want you to tell me. In 1921 you commanded the USS St. Louis, flagship of the Naval Detachment in Turkish waters during the war between Turkey and Greece. Somehow one of your Detachment's small craft got sunk inside Turkish waters. The crew ended up locked up. My father used his considerable influence with the Turkish government to get them released before the situation became a major international incident. When you mentioned repayment he said he would send you a bill, if he ever needed to. I'm here, in his stead."

Quickly Jim outlined the events involving the Purple Hoods.

The Admiral seemed to withdraw into himself for a moment after Jim finished. Jim began to wonder if he was about the get the old heave-ho. Leahy wandered over to his desk and briefly toyed with a couple of mementos on it. Finally the CNO straightened to his full height. An ornate fountain pen in hand, he returned to where Jim stood. He seemed more than a little nervous. The pen twitched almost constantly.

The Old Man looked directly at the Kodachrome print again. He pointed with the pen to a man on one of the stretchers. "Ensign Linsey, now Commander Linsey, skippers a cruiser today, and he'll move up. As did I. Beyond my best hopes. Grumpy old Chief Snarkey there in the stern now runs a bar and grill at Annapolis. All thanks to your father, Mr. Anthony. I'll help you, if I reasonably can.

"Over the last year or two our Intelligence service and criminal investigations people slowly became aware of the group you describe. They are a sub-set of a much larger, law-abiding, group. Their avowed aim is a laudable one. To strengthen the Navy. To make it as powerful and dominating as the British Royal Navy during the age of sail. On the surface the group uses its members, and their families, to lobby Congress for better funding and authorization to rebuild the fleet.

"But a dissident part of them feels that Congress betrayed both the Navy and the country by the drastic cutbacks after The Great War. We do not know exactly how large the group is. Some few of them are officers forced out of the service by those cutbacks. The majority seem to be active duty officers. For muscle they seem to hire those who wish to be in the Navy but do not qualify. They are well funded by certain wealthy families with sons in the service. We know of one case where the group torched a company's research laboratory. Shortly thereafter a project of theirs then in work, or something incredibly similar to it, emerged from one of our facilities. The company had lost all proof that their work even existed. Now, nobody but the United States Navy has a certain device that probably should be shared with our allies. But certain members of Congress will see that it is never shared.

"I don't know what Stubbing Enterprises might have discovered, but it must surely be important. And, I believe they will keep trying to get it. My problem is that I can not be sure who to trust in this matter. For all I know, I may be setting the fox to watch the hen house."

Jim Anthony listened as the Chief of Naval Operations elaborated on the situation. He asked a few questions, but did not receive much additional data in response. Convinced that he had all the information possible from his visit, Jim thanked the Admiral, stepped back into character, and took his leave.

Real professionals are required to take Jim Anthony by surprise. As the door of One Observatory Circle closed behind him the man standing beside the front steps slammed a blackjack against the side of Jim's thin leather motorcycle helmet. Before he could make noise falling, other hands grabbed him. He disappeared in an instant. The man with the sap counted steps to himself as if Jim Anthony still walked toward the Indian at the curb. At just the right timing the motorcycle roared to life. A few seconds later the properly uniformed rider passed under a streetlight before vanishing down the road.

Petty Officer Warren, the CNO's driver watched the operation in open mouthed disbelief. Did someone pull a fast one on the Admiral? Or was the Old Man pulling a fast one? Who would know? Who could he trust? Certainly not his regular chain-of-command. Warren silently slipped away form One Observatory Circle to the secondary road where the staff car lay. Taking advantage of the slight downgrade, he pushed the car to a fast walk. He let the vehicle roll for more than a hundred yards before he slipped the shift lever to first for an almost silent compression start. Via the back roads he headed for Annapolis.

Tom Gentry drove Mephito to the Stubbing brownstone. He had no idea what the old Shaman thought he might find. In a new sweep overnight, the best lab-men of the NYPD discovered nothing new of apparent value. Mephito's face held one of the few expressions Tom easily recognized. Determination.

Inspector Gregg's call ahead got them easy access. Tom held Officer Ziwiki back as Mephito mounted the front stairs. First the old man looked to the skies and began to chant. Then he carefully laid out his fire sticks on the stoop.

As Mephito began to sprinkle on powers from his medicine pouch, the beat cop asked. "What in the world is he doing?"

"I recognize the first part as a prayer for the dead," replied Tom. "Now he's asking for help from the spirits. 'Bout like a Catholic asking a Patron Saint to intervene. There goes the fire and smoke. They show him things."

"Saints preserve us," shivered the cop. "You mean he gets answers?"

"Not always. At least that make sense," said Tom. "But, if he quoted the spirits saying that the sun might come up in the west tomorrow, I'd set my alarm to check the sunrise."

"Well, I'll be... Luck to the both of you. That's scarier than the blamed poison gas."

Tom hurried up the stoop as Mephito beckoned. Together they entered the front door of the brownstone.

After inspecting the main part of the house they entered Gainor's small private room at the back of the second story. Except for a couple of pictures of people in England the room seemed almost sterile.

Finally Tom said, "Jim said Gainor experimented. Wrote articles. There's not even a typewriter here."

Mephito closed his eyes and seemed to test the room with his outstretched hands. "His spirit did not dwell here. Only his body. I feel him both above and below."

They searched the basement. Behind an opulent sitting room, wine cellar, and storage area they discovered an electrical design and work room that rivaled Jim Anthony's own. A closet sized darkroom occupied one corner. "Impressive," muttered Tom.

"There is more, above," replied the old Shaman.

On the top floor, behind Marinda's former play area they found a storage room

"...slammed a blackjack against the side of Jim's thin leather motorcycle helmet."

converted to a book lined study. A small Union Jack stood upon the desk next to a much used Remington portable typewriter. There was even a small window with a view slightly above the brownstone on the other side of the alley. Outside the window sat a small platform containing a nest. As they entered a head poked out of the nest. Piercing eyes looked them over. Then with a high squawk the bird departed.

Tom blinked in surprise, "Peregrine falcon, a female. No wonder there weren't pigeon droppings on the stoop. And look at the little dish outside. Gainor must have fed her."

Mephito grunted. He pointed to a long feather dangling from the ceiling on fishing line. "Feather of the mate, he said.

Never taking his eyes off the feather he dumped the few pieces of paper out of the metal waste basket. He set it directly under the hanging feather. "Quick," he told Tom, "get big canning jar and candle."

Tom returned to the study with an armload of jars, lids, and assorted candles. Without speaking Mephito selected a two quart jar with two piece lid and a plain beeswax candle. He lit the candle, then placed the round jar lid on a ream of typing paper. Pulling a stout knife from his soft leather boots he quickly cut the thin metal from edge to center. Then the old man climbed on a chair set next to the waste basket. It was then Tom noted that a heavy knot now bulged out the fishing line an inch or so above the shaft of the male falcon feather. Looking down he saw the fire sticks in a strange pattern at the bottom of the brass bucket waste basket. He flinched at the amount of powders sprinkled over them.

Holding the lid ring well above the feather, Mephito slid the line into the slot in the jar lid so that it rested on the knot. At a gesture Tom handed him the candle. The Shaman drizzled beeswax to seal the lid airtight. With the lid ring resting on the lid he climbed down.

"Climb up," Mephito told Tom as he handed him the mason jar. "When smoke covers feather screw on jar. Do not touch feather."

"Why did I know this was coming?" Tom asked himself. Mephito's English deteriorated as he became rushed, worried, or excited. Clearly whatever was about to happen meant a lot to the old man.

Tom stood on the chair with one hand gripping the bottom of the big jar. He held the lid with two fingers of the other. He took a deep breath as he saw Mephito ignite a kitchen match with his thumbnail. It was then that he noticed several auburn hairs neatly tied to the fish line and lying along the quill of the feather. A split second later a thick brown and orange smoke enveloped them both.

Petty Officer Ray Warren slipped up the back alley leading to Snarkey's Grill and Grog House in Annapolis Maryland. The Admiral's staff car sat among vehicles awaiting repair a few blocks over. Now in civilian clothes Warren rapped lightly on the Snarkey's kitchen door.

A moment later a grumpy looking face under a mostly gone head of hair looked out.

"Warren, what the Hell are you doing here? Did Uncle Sam kick you out of the Navy?"

"Chief, thank God you're here. I got real trouble. I may even be A.W.O.L., but that's not important."

"Being on French Leave isn't important?" sputtered Snarkey. "You must really be up to your scruffy neck. Come on in. Tell the Chief where the bodies are buried."

Warren gulped, "That's just it, Chief. There may be a body. And either the CNO helped do it, or somebody, maybe his own staff, pulled it off right under his nose. I don't know who to trust. But, I know you still got connections. Please help me figure out what to do."

"Tell me what happened. If it ties in where I think, I do know who can help. Might be dangerous, but who wants to live forever?"

A few minutes later Snarkey made some phone calls. After that a sign saying "Sorry Closed Today" appeared in the place's front window. Then Snarkey, his cook, and Petty Officer Warren, drove away in a battered looking Packard sedan with a surprisingly powerful engine.

Slowly Jim Anthony swam back toward the land of the living. Or at least, the land of the awake. As soon as he realized this he willed his body not to move. Not that he could have moved much with his hands and feet tied to metal stanchions of some kind. Ever so slowly he increased the rate and depth of his breathing. His ears and skin told him he lay on the floor of a high ceilinged cold room. He could hear furtive movements to his left. Things got picked up and set down. Very quietly tools pried and turned. Then a tool slipped on something. Marinda's whispered curse stopped uncompleted.

Carefully Jim allowed his eyelids to open to minute slits. He quickly saw that he rested on the floor of an electrical parts storeroom. The place was long and narrow with heavy shelving along both sides. His hands and feet were shackled to a leg of the shelving system on each side of the aisle. Ripping his bonds loose would bring many hundred weight of junk down on his head.

The fifteen feet to the room's door contained motors, coils of wire, inverters, rectifiers, but no humans. Very slowly he turned his head the other way. Jim's highly exercised peripheral vision just made out Marinda's upper body. She was a mess. Her face held much more grease stains than makeup. Her nice auburn hair seemed to be tied back with copper wire. Her tattered clothing would never come clean. She seemed to be prying something with a screwdriver.

As he turned a bit further he saw a large pile of disassembled electric motors of an out of date design, but no other humans. He watched as she mounted a series of electric motor stator coils one in front of the other on a long piece of heavy wiring "breadboard." The power wires she deftly attached to a series of antique interlocking relays.

Tom drove back to the Waldorf-Anthony as fast as he dared. He knew the Daily Star masthead signs now clipped to the top of the license plates would only buy a semi-blind eye to traffic infractions. The Star heavily backed the Police Department and exposed influence peddlers where ever it found them. But if he got too wild, they'd stop him.

When traffic allowed he glanced over at the Mason jar in Mephito's lap. The old

Shaman's mouth moved in a silent chant. And the feather always pointed in the same direction.

Taking advantage of a fortunate lull in traffic Tom spun the car around to the curb at the side entrance of the hotel, scattering a bevy of reporters. Mephito slid out onto the sidewalk before Tom's hand reached the parking brake. A couple of green reporters called out questions to the old man. The rest stood aside. Strange things seemed to happen to those who blocked the Shaman's way. Tom hurried after Mephito. Tossing the car keys he called, "Hey, Parker. Put the car in the hotel garage. There's a lunch in it for you."

By the time he reached it, Mephito stood in the penthouse's public private elevator. The Bell Captain held the door open while fending off an older man with the same number of stripes on his cuffs. "I am sorry, sir. This car is for the residents only."

"I'm on official business to see Jim Anthony," replied the other. "I can commandeer the car, if I must."

"No you can't, Admiral," interjected Tom. "First, Jim Anthony is not here. Second, be glad you're Navy, not Army. That's Jim Anthony's grandfather you're imposing on. He's a combat veteran who never signed a peace treaty with the U. S. of A. Third, if you even look like you're going for that shoulder holster he'll puncture you like a toy balloon before I could stop him. Assuming I wanted to. And given the last few day's events, 'Anchors Aweigh' is nowhere on our hit music list. Good day, sir."

Tom managed to get the elevator cage shut before the astounded Captain could move. He sent the car up at twice the normal speed.

As the elevator clawed its way upward Tom finally found time to question the old man. "What's that feather pointing to."

Mephito replied, "To what the one spirit wants found."

"And you want to use the auto-gyro to follow its line?"

"Yes."

"Worth a shot," said Tom as he braked the car to a halt. "You grab what you think we might need. I've got to check the craft, the hanger, and the catapult for presents from those purple thugs."

The Shaman nodded sharply as he strode from the elevator.

Jim Anthony's lips did not seem to move, but Marinda heard him clearly. "Are we being watched?"

Marinda's whisper came back. "I haven't found any microphones or peep holes. But there's a shiny new Iconovision television camera, the latest one I've seen, pointed at the area around the door. They turn it around before they come in. Thank heavens you're awake. Someone laid a pretty sizable egg on the side of your head."

"And added some drugs to it, by the way I feel," said Jim as he rolled to face her.

The Packard sedan sped along country roads. Farm fields sped by. CPO Snarkey (retired) commented that the corn and peas went by so fast he saw only Succotash.

After a pause Snarkey asked, "Say Warren, just how did you happen to look me up?"

"I been driving the CNO for the last six weeks," replied Warren. "That's long and weird hours and sometimes even weirder places. And not always stuck out in the parking lot with the car. You pick up things. Scuttlebutt mostly, sure. But not always. Somethin's really been getting under the Old Man's skin. And I don't mean maybe. I've even taken him a few places on the sly. In civvies. More'n once I heard your name mentioned. And its no secret that more'n half the brass stop at your place when they're in 'Napolis. Remember, I was on the St. Louis when you retired. You were the biggest information broker in the whole Atlantic fleet. I didn't figure you'd give that up, even retired. Figured you could point me where I needed to go. Even if you'd really retired."

Soon the Packard turned onto a farm's private drive. Without slowing down they drove past the windbreak of trees, past the farm house, and slid to a halt in the large barn. Snarkey slowly opened the door. He paused, standing on the running board for a moment, the stepped down.

"Stay in the car, you two," he said. "That's for your health. Got it?" With that he climbed the ladder to the hay loft.

Warren could feel more than one pair of eyes on him. He turned to the cook, but the wiry old man seemed asleep.

A couple of minutes later a man with a sidearm appeared from behind a work bench. He did not speak. His arms moved in semaphore code quickly spelling out, "Warren, up the ladder."

Soon Warren climbed into the hay loft. Snarkey directed him to where a man sat with sunlight streaming in behind him. Warren started to raise his hand to his eyes.

"Don't do that, Warren," said Snarkey. "You don't need to see his face. If you trust me, trust him. Tell him your story."

As Tom Gentry finished checking the closed cabin auto-gyro Mephito dropped a canvas bag into the right hand back seat. He fastened his Winchester to clips above the side door. Tom glanced into the bag as the old man lit his fire sticks below the nose of the craft. The canvas sack seemed mostly to contain extra boxes of rifle shells. Mephito placed the jar and feather on the co-pilot's seat, then headed back down stairs.

Tom checked the hangar's doors. He opened them to check the launching rail that would fling the four passenger auto-gyro into the air above New York City's man made canyons. When he returned to start the engine he found a large box strapped to the left hand back seat and a determined old man strapped to the co-pilot's chair.

Tom fired up the auto-gyro's engine. The roar was muted by the best muffler system that Jim Anthony could buy or design. The engine warmed while he checked the sky in all directions. Clear.

As he climbed into the pilot's seat Tom grinned at the irony of the launching system. He and Jim had lifted the concept straight from the Navy. Large ships often carried a small seaplane or two as scouts. Counterweights zipped them into the air from a rail on the ship's deck. At the Waldorf-Anthony Aerodrome the auto-gyro would drop a specially equipped elevator to launch. Tom signaled. Mephito took an even better grip on the precious Mason jar. The engine roared. The elevator dropped. The auto-gyro pinned the two men into their seats as the craft rushed down the rail.

The hotel disappeared beneath them.

"Jim, I'm so sorry. They tricked me like a five year old. I couldn't reach my parents at their usual numbers. There were no messages for me at either service. So I called dad's lawyer. He always knows where dad is headed. He told me the phone couldn't be trusted. He might have something for me in person. I was so worried. I couldn't think of anything but making sure my parents were safe.

"While we were picking out clothes for me Delores showed me the hotel housekeeper's uniform and wig she sometimes uses to sneak in and out of the Waldorf-Anthony. When I got off the phone I made a quick change. I took a cab to the lawyer's office. Three big guys grabbed as I got off the elevator. The lights went out and I woke up here."

Tom kept the auto-gyro low over the New York skyline. Soon Mephito tapped his shoulder. The old man pointed to their line of flight, then to the much different heading suggested by the Falcon feather. Tom reached down and passed the Shaman the headset he should have been wearing.

Intercom ready he said, "I want anybody watching to think we're headed for Washington. That's where we're supposed to think Jim is. That also means our approach will not be from the direction of New York."

Mephito nodded, "Very wise."

Petty Officer Warren winced at some of the sharp questions thrown at him after he finished his story. He answered them without hesitation looking straight at his silhouetted questioner.

The questions ended as the man said, "Thanks, Snarkey. This explains the car that entered the target facility early this morning. Nobody's come out since. This is our chance to catch them with their hands really dirty. Alive or dead, Jim Anthony's a kidnap victim. We move at once. Chief does Warren have what it takes?"

"You wouldn't know to look at him, but I've trusted my back to him in a few very nasty places."

"Right. Warren, I could use another hand, but it's dangerous and you are in no way obligated. Your call."

"I'm in, sir!" replied Warren. "I intend to retire from the Navy. If the Service needs its bilges pumped, I'll be glad to turn to."

"Thank you, Warren. Head downstairs. Chief, tell them to outfit you. I'll be along directly."

As soon as he was alone the man lifted a telephone handset, "Don? We're moving in. You have the perimeter."

"Marinda," whispered Jim Anthony, "can you find a thin piece of something like spring steel? I want to try picking the locks on these shackles."

"You can't," replied the girl. "They poured solder in the key ways."

"I can see and feel that they searched me. Are the heels still on my shoes?"

"Yes. It looks like they tried to pry them off, but couldn't."

Jim sighed, "Finally, a minor break. The hollow heel trick is older than the hills, but I have a variation on it. Are there any heavy tools in here?"

"Sorry, Jim. All the storage areas marked for tools are empty. They overlooked some radio repair kits that had small tools below the meters. I've broken about half of the cheap screwdrivers getting my little project together."

"And just what is that Rube Goldberg's nightmare?"

Marinda actually managed a slight smile before she replied. "Mainly, it's to keep me sane. Working, 'stead of frazzling my nerves worrying. Gainor said he got the diagrams from Hugo Gernsback. They came with a manuscript submitted to Amazing Stories. Basically both of them thought the science had real possibilities, but the fiction had none. And no return postage. So Gainor brought it home. We spent one whole snowy weekend trying to work up a practical design. When I decided to do something to keep my sanity, the idea came back to me like a revelation."

"But does it have a real function? One that might be useful now?" asked Jim.

"If it works, it could be very useful," said Marinda holding up a three foot heavy brass rod with a steel collar around one end. "It's a magnetic catapult."

"That explains a lot," replied Jim as his mind began to race. "I need to get loose. Marinda, please take off my shoes and remove the laces. Now split open one tip of each lace. Good. See the flat metal strip inside each lace? Carefully pull them out. Easy. Easy. Good. Fold them in half, but keep the two strips separate for the moment. They're different materials. Keep folding until they break in half. Lay half of one metal strip on top of one of the other kind. Twist the ends a few times so that the two strips form a sort of cord. Hand that one to me while you prepare the other set the same way."

Jim carefully threaded the "cord" through and around a link in the chain connecting the shackles on his hands. "I see some cotton waste over there. Soak it in some of the water from your pitcher. Now wrap the split ends of the lace to each end of the metal strip here. Get one of my shoes and remove the brand label above the heel inside. Two little plugs came out with it, I hope. Good. Put the wet cotton half under the chain and half over. Push the other ends of the shoelaces no more than an eighth of an inch into the holes you opened in the shoe. Ready? Now avert your eyes, then push the laces all the way in."

A fearful crackling came from within the pile of wet cotton. Light briefly showed through the mass. Jim clenched his teeth as steam flowed over his straining wrists. Then the chain parted.

Jim's arms flew apart. He sat up quickly.

Marinda managed to keep from crying out. Just barely. "What was that, Jim?" she asked. "Thermite?"

"That's right. With a few of my own touches, including magnesium to light it," said Jim. "Now it's time to get to work. Stand back, please."

Marinda withdrew towards the end of the tool room. She watched as Jim Anthony got to his feet. He studied the shelves whose support leg confined the chain linking his ankles. The shelving went almost all the way to the very high ceiling. Each individual shelf contained boxes and other containers, plus various large pieces of electrical gear. Surely he could not be thinking of...

She caught her breath as the big man squatted just enough that his hands could grip the second shelf from the floor. She saw him take a deep breath, then exhale.

Then heave! Muscles beneath his uniform pants stood out like steel cables. The Marine blouse threatened to explode off his body. Then Marinda saw the support leg begin to lift. Ever so slightly at first, then she could see real space under it. Boxes on the shelves quivered and metal housings rattled a bit as the leg rose further still. Finally, Jim transferred the entire load to his right leg. The cords on his neck looked as though they might split the skin. Then Jim's left leg flicked backward, pulling the chain clear. He planted the left leg again to slowly lower the huge mass back into place.

Jim just managed to watch for falling materials as the heavy roaring in his ears returned to something nearly normal. As he hopped to the back of the long room he told Marinda. "Bring the other shoe, the laces, and the other strip. We'll do the other chain where it can't leave a mark on the floor. Then we'll really get to work."

Low enough to get him in trouble with the civil aviation authorities; Tom Gentry circled the small town of Washington Crossing, New Jersey. That circle's radius measured about three-quarters of a mile. He watched the falcon feather rotate as the auto-gyro did. Using the compass and a few local landmarks, he memorized several bearings of the feather. Holding the stick with his knees Tom consulted a map from the large stack always on board.

Soon the auto-gyro touched down in a fallow farm field just outside the city limits. Tom tied down the rotors and drove tie-down stakes to secure the ship. He began to wonder what was keeping Mephito in the cabin. In open mouthed surprise he soon found out.

The Shaman might attract attention, but nobody could possibly connect him to Jim Anthony. Mephito wore a black business suit of a European cut and a Homburg hat. He had loosed his long hair and combed it straight all around. And he carried a cello case, for all the world looking like a misplaced music instructor or orchestra member. Tom had a pretty good idea that the instrument contained in the case played a much different tune than it appeared.

"There's a huge electrical equipment factory just over half a mile that way," Tom told the old man. "It hasn't been used since the Great War ended. The feather points right to the middle of it. Let's go."

Jim Anthony began to place camouflage over something on a high shelf when Marinda urgently whispered, "Jim, the camera is turning!"

Jim dropped to the floor. In an instant he twisted a thin copper wire to hold the chain of the leg shackles together. He lay down so Marinda could do the same for the chain at his hands. The right sleeve of his Marine blouse hid a small breadboard with six tiny switches on it. Marinda managed to connect the cable at his waist to one that ran under the shelves before the camera completed its arc.

From outside the door came an amplified voice, "Miss Stubbing, stand six feet behind Anthony. Keep your hands where we can see them. Anthony, if you try to make any kind of move, we'll gas the both of you. I doubt Miss Stubbing would survive even a mild dose right now."

Jim Anthony knew that the odds were stacked against them. The three catapults he and Marinda managed to cobble together did not have much power. Assuming that his hastily rigged switches all worked properly, they would be of surprise and distraction value only. The last switch should short out the electrical circuit for the room. Moving with all his speed, and in the darkness, he prayed he could get the two of them out of the hands of the Purple Hoods.

A moment later they heard the heavy bolt withdraw. The door swung back only enough to allow two heavyset men in plain purple hoods to enter. One stood with his back against the door. The other took half a step forward.

"Miss Stubbing you will come with us. If you do not cooperate, Anthony will suffer. Maybe die. Now come on."

The fingers of Jim's right hand made the small prearranged signal to begin to cooperate. Marinda slowly walked forward. When she was one step behind him Jim threw the first switch. And all Hell broke loose!

Every light in the room exploded in a shower of sparks like so many flashbulbs. The brass rod sprang from Marinda's first catapult as if shot from a howitzer. Less than a split second later they both heard two thumps, and a hard metallic clack.

In spite of his surprise at the display, Jim Anthony leaped to his feet knowing that the other electrical gizmos would have no power. He hurled himself toward the door, ready to strike or grapple with the two enemies.

Down the corridor a fixture connected to some other electrical circuit remained on. Enough light spilled into the supply room to bring Jim Anthony to an astonished halt. Inches in front of him the first Purple Hood crumpled to the floor. A dark spot on the center of his suit almost looked like an extra button. The man leaning against the door also seem ready to crumple. No chance of that. A few inches of the brass rod gleamed wetly from the lapel pocket of his suit. The other two feet or so, must be inside or behind him.

"Come on, Marinda," urged Jim quietly as he grabbed the sealed breathing devices from the thoroughly dead Purple Hoods.

"What happened?" Marinda whispered as she joined him.

"No idea," replied Jim, as he peered around the tool room door, "but we'd better vacate the immediate area. Stay behind me with one hand touching my back so we don't get separated. If I signal, lock both arms around my neck and hang on for a wild ride."

The empty area outside had the look, and the fading smell of a long disused locker room. Quickly they emerged into a huge open area several stories tall. Only a tiny amount sunlight filtered in from very dirty windows high in the walls. Dimly they could see another structure abutted the wall two hundred feet straight ahead.

Jim looked to the right. Better than a football field away he could barely make out the end of the structure. All the doors there had been bricked over. All over the huge floor sat pads intended to hold heavy machinery. Most stood vacant. A blanket of dust, bits of scrap material and pigeon droppings covered the whole floor. The only footprints led to the left. Reluctantly Jim followed that path, his eyes and ears straining for sounds of approaching trouble.

Marinda followed Jim, confident in his abilities. In the very dim light she alternated between watching the littered floor and the big man's back. Jim stopped.

She felt his muscles freeze. At his signal she threw he arms around his neck and began to pray.

With almost no sound Jim Anthony's legs began to pump like locomotive pistons. He stayed in the well traveled path for about twenty feet until they came even with some sort of dividing wall. Marinda held on for dear life as Jim took a long leap forward while he rotated both of them ninety degrees to face the wall. Jim landed in a deep crouch. Marinda briefly felt her bare knees touch the filthy concrete floor. Then Jim's leg muscles seemed to explode beneath his big body. She actually felt a breeze on her face for a brief instant.

Marinda looked up just as Jim Anthony's fingers barely seemed to gain a purchase on the top of the cinder block wall. His legs folded forward to take up the shock of their bodies slamming into the wall. Or so she thought. Instead Jim's legs rebounded from the wall with such force that her lungs emptied involuntarily. Somehow Jim's fingertips retained their grip on the wall as their two bodies swung in a circle above it.

At their apex Jim managed to rotate them and to switch his grip from one side of the wall to the other. They finished the nearly three hundred and sixty degree orbit of the wall just as Marinda had expected the start of the maneuver to happen. Jim legs absorbed the impact with almost no noise.

Feeling more than a little like Jane in a tree with Tarzan of the Apes, Marinda caught her breath dangling from Jim Anthony's strong neck.

"Men coming down the path," Jim breathed into Marinda's ear. "Let's hope they wipe out my last tracks before they realize we're loose. Quiet now."

Marinda could hear hurried footsteps pass by them through the solid cinder block wall.

Then came a low voice, "Smithers, stay here with the B.A.R. Watch the whole end of this wing for anything moving off the path. Challenge anybody that comes down the path. Even if you're sure it's us. Got that?"

"Understood, sir."

A moment later Marinda rose as Jim Anthony chinned himself for a peek over the wall. Then, with no noise and a minimum of movement, he sat her down on the top of the wall. About fifteen feet towards their former prison stood Smithers. Carrying something that looked like a rifle, he scanned the area they had come from.

Jim put his finger to his lips, then rose to stand atop the wall. Feeling carefully as if to test the wall's stability, he took four sure steps. Then Jim crouched and leaped high toward the guard.

A tiny sound of crunching gravel reached both Marinda and Smithers. The man quickly turned while filling his lungs. He saw nothing because he had not yet looked up. By then it was too late.

Jim Anthony appeared in front of Smithers as if by magic. One hand closed like a spring driven vise on Smither's trigger hand. Marinda just barely saw his eyes fly open in pain and shock. Before a sound could emerge from his mouth, Jim's other fist slammed all the wind out of his lungs. A split instant later a hard driven elbow to the temple ended the struggle. Jim caught the gun as it fell from nerveless hands.

Jim put down the Browning Automatic Rifle. Back opposite Marinda he whispered for her to jump for the path. Seconds later he plucked her out of the air. While Marinda caught her breath, Jim stripped the suit coat and purple hood off of Smithers. He picked the man up by the collar and belt. He cleaned-and-jerked the body, then threw it out of sight behind a tall concrete machine pad.

"Marinda," whispered Jim, "I want to get you out of here to call for help before I take on the rest of the Purple Hoods. But I can't leave that group behind us. You hide behind that set of electrical panels over there. I'll be back as soon as I can."

Marinda watched Jim hurry back down the path. His long strides made so little noise he seemed to be floating. As he stepped to the door of the tool room complex she turned to watch for more trouble coming from the other direction. A moment later she heard a muffled shout from behind her. The sound ended abruptly. Vague noises of chaos continued to drift her way for a time. Then silence.

A short time later Jim Anthony rejoined her. His suit coat was cut or torn in several places. A couple of his knuckles seemed skinned. A brief word and he again led the way along the single path in the debris.

Tom and Mephito kept their bodies behind the trunks of the trees they climbed on the crest of a hill overlooking the huge Fedders Electric Motor Factory. Soon they viewed almost the entire complex through small, but powerful, binoculars.

"Looks to be a fairly easy way in off to the left," said Tom finally.

"Too easy," replied Mephito. "Find another."

Tom did not grumble. The Shaman had forgotten more than he was ever likely to know about stealthy woodcraft and nature in general. Still he kept looking back to the deep swale leading up to the high fence.

"Good place on the south side," said Mephito, "but not good until late afternoon."

"Then t's not good," replied Tom. "Far too late... Wait, I thought I saw something moving where the swale meets the brush line."

Mephito trailed his view back toward the factory. Tom heard him draw a deep breath. "By narrow part of ditch. The sod moves. Like trapdoor spider."

Tom looked at the area just in time to see patches of the heavy grass settling back flush to the ground. "Making sure the hatches work properly, I'll bet." He looked again at the brush. "Somebody getting ready to rush the fence. And they've been detected."

"Enemy of enemy..." Mephito's voice trailed off.

"Damn right! Let's see how fast we can get down there."

Chief Petty Officer (retired) Don Snarkey hated the woods. What am I doing this far inland, he asked himself. He felt like he was locked in a rat infested cargo hold. On the other hand, his cook, Ruben Clampett, the Arkansas mountaineer, put on this "wilderness" like an old glove. For the hundredth time Snarkey wondered what wanderlust made him into a fine sailor. Now he carried a Springfield '03 rifle like it was part of his body. With Warren, Snarkey's contingent brought the infiltration team to eight.

Their scouts now hid in the shadows of the gully that paralleled the Fedders Factory fence for a time. Then Ruben's turn came. Without seeming to move much at all he joined the scouts in an amazingly short time. Now me, thought Snarkey, I'll probably fall into a hidden cache of pots and pans and sound louder than a brass band. Neptune, help me, here I go.

Tom and Mephito crawled like crazy through the two foot high unmowed green hay that extended to the edge of the swale. They slowed way down about twenty yards out. Somehow Mephito managed to bring the cello case along. Now he opened it. He passed Tom goggles, a small gas mask, and a handful of Jim's hastily made purple gas antidote spheres. Quietly he worked the lever of the old Winchester to chamber a round. Then came the edged weapons.

Snarkey breathed a sigh of relief as the last man joined them. He rechecked his .45 automatic before slipping a set of brass knuckles onto his left hand. They had traveled about fifteen yards when Snarkey heard a muffled cry of "NOW!"

On the side of the gully away from the factory six sections of the long vegetation flipped backward. From each hole one or more men in Purple Hoods rose with to point weapons at them.

The hooded man with a small flame painted on his hood called out, "Surrender, or..."

That's as far as he got. Something glanced off his head with a dull thud. He pitched out of the hole into the gully. The remaining Purple Hoods paused as if waiting for someone to take charge. Not a long pause, but any pause turned out to be far too long.

Tom flipped his automatic back to his right hand as soon as the rock left it. He hurried forward before the Hoods could turn around. "Don't shoot," he called out as he reached the spot between the first two holes. Two men turned to meet him. One held a gas gun. The other brought up an automatic. Tom pistol whipped the one with the gas gun. The other took a Comanche war arrow between the eyes.

Tom ducked as he moved to the third hole. Two of the Hoods stood back to back. One covered the gully as the other tried to find Mephito in the grass. Of all things, a French knife flashed up from the gully as the old Shaman's second arrow flew true. Tom hurdled over the hole as they fell. At the fourth hole he threw in two spheres. The Purple Hood there disappeared in a cloud of white.

A bald man from the gully scrambled into that hole. A brief struggle ensued. By then the men from the gully poured into the last holes. The fight ended quickly.

Again, Jim led the way down the path in the dust.

A wide eyed Chief Snarkey dusted the white powder off of his clothes as he took in the party of two that staged his group's timely rescue. The one in aviator's togs he understood. The wiry old man who tossed a cello case into the gully before vaulting down baffled him. He carried a short bow in one hand and a cowboy's rifle in the other. His coat spread open as he fell. Snarkey couldn't count the metallic things attached to the lining.

The aviator and the team's leader began a quiet conference to one side. Beside him Ruben pulled the heavy French knife out of the fallen Purple Hood.

"Whew, doggies, my nephew Jedidiah always tells me that this is a sissy knife," said the mountaineer. Then he noticed Mephito's medicine pouch. "Thanks a heap for the help, Shaman. By those markings you're probably not Cherokee."

"No," replied the old man, "Comanche. Are you of the Cherokee?"

"By blood, no," smiled Ruben, "but my family has been proud to be honorary Cherokee since before the Trail of Tears."

A smile cracked through the wrinkles around the old man's mouth. He nodded sharply, then offered Ruben his hand.

Marinda tossed two more gas guns into the improvised sack she carried.

Jim's flying feet put two charging Purple Hoods on the ground like they were standing still. And almost silently. Her Vassar French teacher once showed the class a French Apache film that featured moves like Jim's.

She retied the cord around the top of the looted purple hood. That cloth was now so full that she looked like she carried the severed head of an enemy.

Very little of the huge factory seemed to have power. When they approached these last two, one man had been trying unsuccessfully to use an old telephone. A moment later Jim and Marinda entered an area sealed off with canvas from the rest of the factory. Here the floors were clean. New tables and benches held mostly modern machines and equipment. Apparently Jim had just taken out the guards that secured the rear of the active area.

They spent a very brief time looking at the machinery and the work benches illuminated by battery powered emergency lights. When they zipped the canvas door behind them they entered another hundred yard stretch of filthy, stripped down factory area. By now Marinda feared that the only working doors to the whole complex must be at the Purple Hoods' headquarters.

Their path ran near the left wall. Soon a lesser traveled path veered off to their right. Keeping low Jim and Marinda followed it until they could see the path's end. Against the right wall sat another one of those walled off areas. This one was guarded. A single Purple Hood paced around the front wall of the structure. To one side of the barred door sat a table with a kerosene lantern and empty food trays. Three of them.

"Prisoners," whispered Jim. "Are you game to be another one?"

Snarkey could tell the aviator and his leader needed to work out a thing or two. This unholy mess involved a lot of deception. Snarkey's jaw almost hit his breastbone when his boss allowed the fly boy to check his face for a possible mask. But he trusted the leader. And more, he trusted Ruben Clampett's instincts. In twenty years he'd never seen the man shake hands with anybody he could not trust.

A moment later Snarkey watched the old Indian lean the cello case against the gully wall and climb into the enemy's fighting position. He followed.

A certain Purple Hood felt really alone in the factory. Just lucky he had that old lantern, or he'd be nearly in the dark. He spun around as he heard footsteps approaching.

"You're hurting my arm," came an anguished female voice from the path.

Then he could see one of his mess mates nearly dragging a young woman along.

"Can't hold her back there anymore. Got to secure her here," came an authoritative voice.

The guard started to pull the key from his pocket as they approached. Then he remembered the proper procedure. He asked "By whose order?"

He heard the word "Mine!" just as he saw more fireworks than on the Fourth of July.

Moving through the narrow tunnel leading to the factory Tom Gentry felt secure with his new companions. He believed the leader's story. As importantly, maybe more so, loomed Mephito's handshake with that knife throwing scarecrow. That didn't happen unless the Shaman felt he could trust the man. Tom smiled under his purple hood.

"Marinda, remember to keep quiet," Jim Anthony cautioned as he put the guard's key in the door's lock. The room inside had no light at all. Jim moved the kerosene lantern so its light spilled into the room.

"Mom! Dad!" Marinda managed to keep her voice to a fierce whisper. "I've been so worried."

The Purple Hoods had not been gentle with the older Stubbings. The father showed signs of a pretty thorough beating. The mother seemed better off, but she had obviously been slapped around more than a little.

Jim kept watch as the Stubbings accessed each other's condition. Finally Robert Stubbing asked, "Marinda, do you know anything about this calculation device these fiends keep asking about?"

"Gainor was trying to perfect it for a descendant of Charles Babbage." Marinda repeated what she told Jim earlier. "Their families are close. He let me borrow it to show Dr. Hopper. Now Gainor is dead and we're in all this trouble."

"That's enough for now," interjected Jim Anthony. "We need to find a good place to hide you until its safe to leave."

It's the Purloined Letter all over again, thought Jim as he headed for the main path. Only this letter's armed. Robert Stubbing knew how to use the captured B.A.R. Marinda's hood full of weapons contained three Colt .45 automatics belonging to unfortunate team leaders. Surprisingly, Alicia Stubbing deftly chambered a round in each of the pistols and announced them ready to fire. The reunited Stubbing family sat invisibly at the back of the roof of the former cell. Now I can really get to work, thought Jim.

In what had once been the executive offices of the sprawling plant a hooded man stood at a portable switchboard. "Sabotage," he exclaimed out loud. "It has to be sabotage." Electricity remained in the next room where he slept, but most of the rest of the offices had only sunlight to see by. He touched the large flame on his hood's forehead. He sent for the Stubbing girl some time ago. That would take the starch out of her father. Before the detail could return the lights flashed bright, then blew out. The south window to the factory floor showed smoke rising from the power distribution room.

As he checked his weapons he decided the time had come to cut losses. Just like those supposed friends and allies cut themselves free of their debt from the Great War. He hurried out to the factory floor.

The battle for the tunnel gate ended quickly. The deception of wearing the "uniform" of the Purple Hoods lasted just long enough. One falling thug managed

"...he saw more fireworks than the Fourth of July."

to fire a single gas round. The devilish thing burst on the cheekbone of the one unhooded man as he entered the fray. Tom turned and threw a sphere at the man's feet. So did Mephito as Chief Snarkey's brogan nearly took the shooter's head off.

All purple vanished in the twin white clouds. Quickly Mephito began applying an herbal astringent to the bleeding cuts on the man's face. Tom knew well the effectiveness of the preparation. And no germ could live through it.

Ruben Clampett commented, "His head's ringing like Eight Bells of the watch, but he'll be fine."

Leaving the wounded man to guard the tunnel entrance they entered the factory floor. Nothing in sight moved. Off to the right stood an Army GP Large tent. Weapons ready, the scouts entered.

"Billets," came the report. "Nobody home, but we found this."

He produced a map of the complex.

As Jim Anthony approached an Army style tent, he heard footsteps coming from one side of a cross-path and noted a flashlight in the other direction. He made one of the longest standing broad jumps in history to disappear behind a machine pad. He peeked around the pad's corner. The man with the flashlight seemed to march, rather than walk. The two from the other direction came to attention two paces in front of him.

"Set the scuttling charges. Then head for the perimeter exits," said the man with the large flame painted on his hood. The two in plain hoods saluted and headed off. The high ranking Purple Hood did an about face to return the way he came.

Jim desperately wanted to go after the probable leader of the operation. On his own he might well have. With the Stubbings and possibly others in danger, he cut across the factory floor after the subordinates. He knew that scuttling charges were used to sink warships to keep secrets from enemy hands. In this case evidence needed to go to Davy Jones' Locker, including some still alive.

Tom followed the Navy team leader toward the two story office complex within the center section of the factory. The map marked it as HQ. A gun roared by a door into the place. Tom felt the bullet split the air between the two of them. The leader tried to say "Return fire!" Before he finished the first word the Winchester's larger bellow drowned him out. Mephito sent a lead messenger into the space just vacated by the shooter.

The team sought cover as alternating fire from a group of windows of the offices sought them.

"One man, two guns," said Tom.

"Agreed," said the leader. "Suppressing fire!"

Quickly pistol fire began shattering the glass facing them. It was not returned. A few seconds later a klaxon horn began to sound.

Mephito spoke up, "He moves away."

"I agree, sir," came Ruben's voice.

"That alarm's 'Abandon Ship.' Advance to the flanking areas."

One of the Purple Hoods hurried as he worked the combination lock on the rusting electrical panel. After he threw the four switches he would be glad to run for the hills. And the Devil take the hindmost! The lock released and slid off. Before he could remove the shackle from the door loops something struck his hands like a pile driver.

The random sounds of the lock served to cover the small noises Jim Anthony made with his approach from the side. As he saw the lock begin to slide he knew he could not afford to let the door open. Out of the darkness he leaped, feet forward, legs folded. Less than three feet away his legs exploded forward.

Lock dropping from his numb hand, the Purple Hood spun around, his face a mask of agony. Nobody would ever count the broken bones in his hand and forearms. He died when his head slammed into that of his companion.

With the two thugs down in a heap Jim turned to the dangerous panel box. No time to try disarming the infernal device, he decided. Jim grasped the two ends of the shackle still holding the door closed. In an instant he used the training of his Eastern instructors to fuse the strength of the Comanche with the stubborn determination of the Irish. His hands moved convulsively. Jim's hands bled a bit as he hurried to where he thought the senior Purple Hood might be. The shackle now needed to be cut off.

The Navy's augmented assault team swept through the lower floor of the factory offices. The place showed signs of occupancy. They could not move very fast as they checked every nook and cranny for hidden enemies and explosive traps. Finally only a large conference room remained.

They silently opened the double doors on one side of the room. One man moved out each way along the wall. The rest of the team entered just as a fierce kick propelled the door opposite them into the center of the room. A single, very large, Purple Hood took a long rolling dive into the room.

Instinctively Tom grabbed the team leader's arm as he shouted a strange word. Ruben Clampett froze as the Shaman's hand appeared in front of his face. Mephito, too, called out.

The large man continued to roll, but somehow the hood vanished. The team leader yelled, "Hold fire! That's Jim Anthony!"

With all hoods off, the leader of the Navy team began, "I know you have reason to be suspicious of me..."

"Not anymore, Mr. Ventnor," replied Jim. "Admiral Leahy personally vouched for you. I guess he just didn't know how deeply his household staff was involved."

"But how?" replied the real Harmon Ventnor. "Warren told us the CNO only gave a very basic outline of the problem."

"Leahy outfoxed him, too," replied Jim. "He toyed with objects on his desk. He used a model signal light to ask if I knew Morse Code. After I acknowledged he stood close to me gently tapping away with a fountain pen. I barely heard it. He signaled 'Ventnor is alive. Trust him.' and 'Go to Snarkey for more.' Of course I hit a detour leaving."

"Mr. Anthony, let's finish cleaning out this place."

With the first floor clear, the team stood at the bottom of the only staircase to the second level.

"Trap," said Mephito.

"We might be safer scaling the outside wall," began Ventnor. He stopped as they heard a strangled grunt from above. A safe about three feet on a side appeared at the top of the stairs. The leading wheels dropped over the edge. A final shove sent the whole thing over. Men dove for cover. Most did not see the small round object bounced down the stairs after the safe.

"Mills Bomb!" shouted Jim. He leaped over the safe as it embedded one edge into the ground floor. Jim got his fingers under the edge of the safe as he watched the English hand grenade bounce down the last few steps. As it hit the last tread he heaved.

The safe tipped over as Jim folded his body as small as possible on what became the top side. The opposite side came down on the Mills Bomb. Jim never knew if the timer triggered the thing or the weight of the safe did it. He rode out the blast with fingers crammed in his ears.

As soon as the safe settled Jim leaped up the stairs. As the others soon followed another explosion came from outside the factory walls. Hanging from an outside window was a rope ladder. Below dust billowed up from the mouth of a collapsing tunnel.

Glumly the team began a search of the upper floor. Soon came the yell of "Someone's in here."

A door was forced open. Behind it sat Commander Hershell chained to a ring in the floor.

Words came in a flood, "They impersonated me. Later the kidnapped me. I don't know what they wanted..."

The hands helping Hershell froze when Jim Anthony declared, "Save the lies, Hershell. You've been impersonating yourself. I've used that type of mask a time or two. I measured the one you took off at Vassar with a micrometer. It covered your features, but didn't disguise the shape of your face at all. The trick just gave you a convenient out if you were suspected. And that day it helped you shed the white powder."

"Y-y-you can't be serious," protested Hershell.

"Deadly serious," said Jim grimly. "The white powder has chemical markers in it. Tom, do you have the testing reagent?"

"Right here. Catch."

"Hershell, traces of the powder will still be in your eyes. With one drop of this the green color around your eyes will prove you were at Vassar!"

Hershell screamed. He yanked a knife free from his belt buckle. With a slash across one seaman's arm he dived for a nearby field desk. His hand pulled out another Mills Bomb.

Mephito's Winchester roared. The bullet shattered Hershell's forearm. The unarmed grenade rolled away.

As he started to go back to get the Stubbings Jim Anthony said quietly, "You'd better start talking. My grandfather is not in a good mood."

Jim helped support Robert Stubbing as they entered the first floor conference room, now apparently a command post.

A man Jim had not seen before entered and saluted Ventnor. "Commander Winslow's compliments, sir. Parameter secure. Several men in custody."

"Very well," replied Ventnor. "Phone Ensign Sawyer to clean out One Observatory Circle. Mr. and Mrs. Stubbing, thank the Lord you two are not seriously hurt. Medical help is set up in the next room."

Shortly Marinda returned. "The medic says nothing is very serious. They just want to rest."

"Excellent," said Ventnor. "We'll try to get your statement as soon as possible. We'll also need your friend's statement, Mr. Anthony. He went out to find the source of the electrical problems."

As if on cue, Tom Gentry came into the room. His face held a really bemused look. "Jim," he said with almost a sigh in his voice, "I found the power distribution controls for this whole wing of the factory. You are not going to believe it."

"Believe what?" asked Jim.

"Come see for yourself. You really need to."

Jim, Marinda, and Mephito followed Tom through cavernous areas of the empty electric motor factory. Scraps of many kinds of material crunched under their feet. Copper gleamed beside weathered insulation, and chunks of Bakelite.

"That walled off area ahead is where we're going," said Tom.

"Looks like the debris around the room was hit by a tiny whirlwind," observed Jim.

"But, you'll notice that there is only one set of fresh footprints going to the door. Mine."

Inside the open topped room stood a huge metal device with a heavy wooden table in front of it. The table mounted an array of three armed knife switches. The room smelled of hot metal and scorched wood. Lines of char on the wood led from terminal to terminal to terminal. Here and there in those still smoking channels lay metal beads.

Jim's quickly analyzed the lines. So did Marinda.

"Jim, this setup is quite old, but isn't this the transformer system from the utility high tension lines? I thought so. And this board sent out the various voltages and cycle rates to the machinery in this huge area. I think everything coming in got shorted into the tool room."

"I agree, Marinda. Anything smaller that a ten gauge wire would have nearly vaporized under the load."

"But, where are the wires that caused this?" replied Marinda.

"I don't know. The connector cables hanging over there would make the job easy, but they're covered with dust."

"Jim, did you happen to notice what's missing from the floor around here?" asked Tom.

"Missing? Howling Coyotes! That whirlwind. The copper scrap."

"That's right, old friend. Bit by bit the copper was placed across those burned areas. Then a bigger piece completed the circuit. And without leaving tracks."

"But how...?" began Jim.

A low chuckle from Mephito stopped him. The old Shaman reached to the floor on one side of the table. "Here are the tracks," he said as he cupped something in his hand.

Jim, Tom, and Marinda gathered around. Nestled in the old man's palms were three feathers.

Marinda's eyes flew open. "Excalibur!" she exclaimed.

"The Peregrine's mate?" said Tom.

"What?" said Jim Anthony.

"Those are Excalibur's feathers," said Marinda firmly. "He's a Peregrine Falcon that fell out of the nest behind our brownstone. Gainor hand raised him, with a little help from me. He and his mate now live in the alley. His scallop and a half flight feather markings are unique. But how..."

In Comanche Jim Anthony quietly asked Mephito, "Gainor's spirit took the falcon over?"

"I doubt that, grandson. Probably the bird just repaid the spirit for all the kindness shown to him."

The End

ALL FOR CHARITY
My Original Title

This story takes place about four years ahead of Jim Anthony's first recorded adventure in Super-Detective. I wrote it before I had the chance to read any of the trilogy that begins the Big Boy Scout's™ original series. I have now read the "Dealer In Death," the first novel and have the other two parts on hand. Dealer is far more like an early Doc Savage story than I expected. The later stories are less epic, but more fun. I hope I've achieved a good blend of Jim's two adventure types. I also hope I have not used any elements that were introduced in the second and third stories.

In my opinion, of all the public domain hero-pulp characters, Jim Anthony better lends himself to stories for the modern reader than any other. At least that I can think of. And for one reason. His Native American heritage means that he will not automatically believe in the motives of government employees. Of course he will cooperate and assist, but not blindly. He will judge government officials he meets as individuals, not by the alphabet soup of their employer's initials. (And for context, it is now a matter of public record that J. Edgar Hoover took offense and intervened when portrayals of G-Men was not to his liking. This lasted from the early radio *Green Hornet* to TV's *Hawaii-50* in the 1960's.)

Warning: Possible spoilers below!

I was visiting Orlando, Florida, in October 2007 when I began this story. The idea started out: a perturbed Jim Anthony being sold for charity. Well, an evening on the town with him, anyway. That was going to get mixed in with what perturbed him. Then I decided that the intruders in the Stubbing household wore purple hoods. I never got back to figuring out what was bothering Jim on page one.

What I did not find out, until Christmas, was that a close family friend had participated in a nearly identical charity event in Kansas City at roughly the same time I wrote the beginning of the story.

Another event in Orlando contributed to this story. One evening the wife and I went to the Nightwalk at the Universal Studios park. On the way in we kept seeing people holding signs that said *"Grace Hopper."* Now the late Dr. Grace Hopper was one of the pioneers of the computer age. She retired from the U.S. Navy a Rear Admiral. Some may remember her from interviews on Sixty Minutes. She often handed out cut pieces of wire representing Micro-, Milli-, and Pico-Seconds. Finally

I asked one of the people with the signs what was going on. Seems a group of women from the technical fields was having their annual meeting that week in Dr. Hopper's name.

When grad student Marinda Stubbing needed a mentor I did some checking. In 1937 Grace Hopper, PhD, served on the Vassar College faculty. Bingo! And she may also be the reason the Navy crept into the story.

Other real people and places involved in this story:

Jimmy Durante, one of the great American entertainers. Singer, comic, actor. One of his acting roles was as the very pulpish manager of the movie version of Joe Palooka.

Alfred Lunt & Lynn Fontanne, the royal couple of Broadway for many decades. The net makes it easy to find out what was playing on the Great White Way whenever I place a story.

Charles Babbage has a great Wikipedia entry explaining his mechanical calculation engines.

Admiral William D. Leahy, Chief of Navel Operations in 1937. His career is on the public record. I just sank one of his small boats in 1920 or so.

About **Number One Observatory Circle** the Wikipedia says: "Located on the grounds of the United States Naval Observatory in Washington, D.C., the house was built in 1893 for its superintendent. The Chief of Naval Operations (CNO) liked the house so much that in 1923 he took over the house for himself. It remained the residence of the CNO until 1974, when Congress authorized its transformation to an official residence for the Vice President."

For the story's final battle I looked at maps for something more or less between New York City and Annapolis, Maryland. The name **Washington Crossing, New Jersey**, just seemed to jump off the screen. And it was in the right place. Problem solved.

Dawkins' "narration voice" and the description of the food is a tip of the hat to a character created by Charles Merril Smith in the *Reverend Randollph* mysteries. Introduced in the second book of the series, Clarence Higby is a Cockney master chef who is often asked to enlighten those served about what they are eating. About halfway between pulp and genteel detective stories, former Rams quarterback the Reverend Dr. C.P. Randollph pastors a church in a Chicago Loop high rise building and solves murders, usually with a religious history aspect of one kind or another. I wish there had been more than the six books that make up this series.

The Purple Hoods may well return. I know that I expect to return to Jim Anthony at some point. And when I do, Dawkins' history as an intelligence agent, from the second original story, will play at least some part. Also, expect to learn the origin of that "short bow" that Mephito carries.

ERWIN K. ROBERTS - had not yet learned to read as the last days of the pulps unfolded. His family started his life long interest in adventure stories by reading to him Kipling, *The Swiss Family Robinson*, volumes of *Doctor Dolittle*, along with tales of *Robin Hood* and *Thor* illustrated by the legendary N.C. Wyeth. On the radio he discovered *Space Patrol, Big John & Sparky*, and of course *The Lone Ranger*. When the family went to the movies they were most often Westerns and Swashbucklers.

When his own children were young Erwin hurried home from work so that he could watch *Duck Tales* with them.

For fifteen years Erwin produced, edited, wrote, occasionally directed, and appeared about 1000 times on access/community cable TV in the Kansas City area. For a brief time he hosted the WBE-TV network's national *Action Theater* as *Major A.D. Venture*.

These days Erwin writes pulp hero stories about some of the classic characters, as well as his own, more contemporary, characters.

His novel of the first of a new generation of Independent Operators *"Plutonium Nightmare"* is available at http://www.lulu.com/modern-knights. About the book Ron Fortier said, in part: "Enter the mysterious, no-face hero known by the police and public only as The Voice. Once again the pulse-pounding beat of classic pulp adventures is sounded, only this time in a more modern setting. And it all works. Roberts obviously knows pulps and captures their break-neck pacing perfectly, while at the same time adding in a heavy does of bloody, shoot-em-up action."

On the horizon is more of *The Voice*, plus heroic stories set in the 21st century detailing *The Journey of Freedom's Spirit & Samuel*. Watch for them.

Erwin K. Roberts can be reached at erwin.k.roberts@gmail.com

JIM ANTHONY

in

DEATH WALKS BEHIND YOU

By Andrew Salmon

Chapter 1

Orson Woolcott III was scared.

Now it seems unlikely that one of the world's wealthiest industrialists had anything to be particularly scared of. Mining, shipping, construction, oil – all these Woolcott ruled with an iron fist. And yet, as Orson Woolcott III hurried along the short block from his lavish penthouse across from Central Park, the hair stood up on the back of his neck. His shoulders hunched as though braced for a blow as his mad eyes darted left and right, seeing murder lurking in every shadow. For a man with his finger on the pulse of the world, it was strange that a mere telegram was the cause of his distress. A telegram whose message contained four simple words, words which froze the blood of Woolcott:

Death walks behind you.

This had been the message. A brief missive that had kept Orson Woolcott III locked in his rooms like a death row inmate for more days than he cared to think about. Telephones had been brought in for him to exert his will around the globe. Teletypes as well. Food needed to be prepared by New York's finest chefs and delivered to his prison aerie. And only his most trusted allies were granted admittance. Staff, organs of his will -- these were the underlings he used to extend the influence of Woolcott Enterprises far and near.

But on this particular evening, Orson Woolcott III walked alone.

For sixteen days and nights, he'd ruled from on high. For sixteen days and nights he'd eaten lukewarm delicacies, slept in the same bed, stared at the same wallpaper and breathed the same air. And he simply couldn't stand it any longer. To a man used to having the world at his beck and call, the expansive rooms of his penthouse seemed to shrink daily, squeezing the life out of him.

Until this night.

Fog had rolled in, obscuring everything in an enveloping gray. Woolcott, peering from his window earlier had watched the fog descend while his underlings had prattled on about daily affairs. When he could no longer see the street below, he had driven them from his rooms, dressed in his finest tails and top hat and stealthily rode the elevator down.

Mollari's, New York's finest steak house was directly across the street from the hotel. The eatery had been one of many seeing to Woolcott's culinary cravings over the term of his self-imposed captivity. But tonight he would dine in style. At his regular table for all the world to see.

The Crimson Scorpion could go hang.

For it had been that agent of evil who had dispatched the telegram to Orson Woolcott III.

Three other wealthy industrialists had met their deaths after receiving a simple epistle with that chilling handful of words: *death walks behind you.*

All three had died horribly.

Daniel Dickson Bellamy had been slain aboard the Princess, the pride of his steamship line.

Maxwell Faust had perished on his ranch while hosting a sweet sixteen party for his niece.

Humphrey J. Stackpole had been struck down while walking the very streets Woolcott careened down now.

Death walks behind you.

Woolcott heard the phrase in his mind and quickened his pace. It was a phrase repeated in harsh whispers at every board meeting and hissed through the clenched lips of the elite at every gentleman's club since Bellamy had fallen to the Crimson Scorpion. Woolcott's earlier bravado, jarred momentarily by these ominous recollections, was slow returning as he waited for the traffic signal to change. A crowd of pedestrians pressed around at the curb. In the smothering fog, they appeared ghostly, faceless as they surrounded him, their plummed breath tickling his ears from behind.

The light changed at that moment and Orson Woolcott III dashed across the street, his head hunched down in his cashmere overcoat.

He was being silly he knew.

Woolcott Enterprises moved mountains. Who was he to fear some nut calling himself the Crimson Scorpion? Bellamy. Faust. Stackpole. Movers of mountains in their own right. The names sent shivers down his spine. But Mollari's was just ahead. He had made it. He gloated to himself that he had outsmarted his unseen foe. He had craved what passed for fresh air in the city and a hot meal. And what Orson Woolcott III wants, he gets. Crimson Scorpion or no. Cryptic telegrams be damned. He would dine then return to his rooms a new man, refreshed from his exercise and invigorated with triumph.

He saw the warm glow of Mollari's bay window tingeing the fog a soft yellow. The doorman, a portly fellow, acknowledged Woolcott with the briefest of nods and turned to open the black oak door of the eatery. The rich man stepped lightly towards his destination, even putting a swing to his arms as he savored his victory.

Mere inches from crossing the threshold, his left arm swung back. Woolcott felt a slight sensation along the base of his palm, like a scratch -- so faint as to be almost undetectable. He shrugged it off as mild contact with one of the lower ranks behind him.

Behind?

Nonsense. He was safe. Mollari's was warm, cozy, inviting. He stepped inside. The steward took Woolcott's coat, hat and cane. Woolcott shot his cuffs and prepared to make his entrance. He wanted to look his best when his competition for wealth and power saw him enter the restaurant. Oh, many of the elite were too afraid of this ridiculous Crimson Scorpion, but they had representatives there to eavesdrop on the rich and powerful who disdained any sign of weakness or temerity. Woolcott's right hand tugged his left cuff, the back of his right hand came away with a single drop of his blood above the knuckle of his index finger. Puzzled, Woolcott examined the hand but found no source for the blood.

He looked at his left hand. There was a faint scratch, half an inch long, arched like a crimson, toothless grin leering up at him.

Then things began to happen quickly.

First he felt overheated. He was burning up as if he stood outside the gates of Hell. His mouth went bone dry while chills chased each other up and down his spine. There was a swelling sensation. The tight-lipped crimson grin burst open like a tiny mouth braying laughter. But what came out was anything but amusing. Woolcott's precious blood, not blue but all too red, poured out of him. He watched in horror as more tiny, evil mouths broke into fleshy grins all over his powdered skin. Blood rained down onto the black and white mosaic spelling out the restaurant's name on the floor.

The steward gawped in shock, then sent the hatcheck girl for the manager. In the time it took for the steward to bark his commands, Orson Woolcott III had become a fountain of blood streaming down from every inch of his body.

With a wet, helpless groan, he staggered and splashed onto the floor, crimson gore flying from the impact to splatter the onlookers who had gathered in response to the steward's action. Oozing pustules followed the streaming blood. Agonizing spasms shook Woolcott's deformed body. He tried to scream but his tongue was horny and swollen with livid sores. It lasted bare minutes but for Orson Woolcott III it seemed to take eons. And every last second of his life ticked away in searing pain.

When death came it was a relief.

Chapter 2

The Waldorf-Anthony Hotel soars forty-four stories above the busiest street in the world. It stands as a black and chromium testament to man's ingenuity. It is home to at least one hundred clubs where adventurers from every corner of the globe meet to trade tales of incomparable daring. And during these boisterous sessions, men long accustomed to the grand wonders and perilous secrets of the world always speak of one name with awe. This man's name garners such admiration not because he was the major stockholder in the hotel that bore his name and not solely because he had his headquarters in Penthouse A. Rather these rough adventurers knew that the man in Penthouse A was Jim Anthony.

Recognized throughout the world as a man of epic abilities, Jim dedicated his life to solving crimes in the never-ending quest to satiate his ceaseless, probing curiosity.

But little did Jim Anthony know that his greatest adventure was set to begin as he glided back to the Waldorf-Anthony.

Fog had greeted Jim and his associates upon their arrival from The Pueblo – his secluded oasis deep in the Mojave where the internationally acclaimed athlete and crime solver periodically retreated from the prying eyes of the world. The fog had stayed with them, giving Tom Gentry a double dose of the fits. For you see, Tom served not only as Jim's chauffeur, trained agent and right hand man, but was also Anthony's pilot. Thus he had battled the fog while guiding Jim's Douglass plane, Thunderbird, down to earth but now fought the smothering shroud of gray through narrow streets choked with traffic. It was with a sigh of relief that Tom Gentry pulled the limousine up to the curb outside the Waldorf-Anthony. He pawed the sweat from his broad, freckled forehead and blew air out of pursed lips.

"Golly, I'm glad that's over," he said with a shake of his large head. "I'd'a sooner faced a herd of stampedin' rhinos than that unruly lot." He gestured at the traffic.

Jim ignored his friend's outburst. He had sprang out of the car before it had stopped moving and was already conducting his fiancé, Delores Colquitt, out of the back seat. Behind her hunched Mephito. Mephito was Anthony's grandfather. The withered Comanche Shaman resembled a blackened, living skeleton emerging from the gloom behind blond, blue-eyed Delores.

Mephito stepped down to the sidewalk, his probing eyes staring straight ahead. His gnarled hands, veined with age, hovered near a grimy buckskin bag hung at his skinny waist. Inside were nine Shaman sticks old Mephito used to divine the future much to the chagrin of Gentry who held no truck with mysticism.

With Jim Anthony and party clear, Tom tooled the car towards the underground parking garage. The doorman stepped forward to herald the return of the distinguished permanent resident with a tip of his cap.

It was at that moment they heard the screams coming from the adjacent block.

These screams were immediately followed by more screams, car horns blatting and the squeal of hastily applied brakes.

"Jim, whatever could be happening?" Delores asked, her gaze riveted on the corner where the noise seemed to be issuing.

There was no answer from her betrothed. She pulled her eyes off the sight of people dashing for their lives and looked to Jim for answers.

Jim Anthony was gone.

She flung her gaze about, searching, before spotting Jim's unruly mop of black hair and the granite wedge of his back cutting efficiently through the panicked masses. Not away from the disturbance, but directly towards it!

She called futilely after him, then stamped her foot in frustration. "Why does he do it? Why does he imperil himself so?"

The fleeing crowd was threatening to overtake them and in their mad haste would not hesitate to trample them underfoot. Mephito fingered his Shaman's bag, then, without a word, led Delores inside to safety.

Chapter 3

When Jim arrived outside Mollari's, he found a scene of chaos and confusion. The police arrived just as he did and began unceremoniously shoving the crowd back from the entrance. The crowd seemed split between those anxious to flee and those desperate to gawk. Jim squared his mighty shoulders and dove into their midst. At first he was met with resistance but gradually, as more and more of the pedestrians recognized him, the crowd parted and he was able to reach the entrance.

His hyper keen senses took over, flooding information into his razor sharp intellect. First was a scent of something in the air -- something out of the ordinary for a busy New York street. The presence of this odor was a mystery to him until he saw the sprawled, bloody body laying in the entranceway to the restaurant. One of the constables shifted the sheet in order for the arriving detective to view the body. The crowd saw more than they bargained for and gasped, rearing back. Jim leaned closer, his piercing gaze missed nothing. The sheet dropped into place a second later, but Anthony had seen all he needed to see.

Over the heads of the teeming throng he spotted the out of shape hat of Lieutenant Carothers. The big man was directing his men to cordon off the body and move the gawkers along.

"Carothers!" Jim yelled, gliding through the crowd. "Clear everyone out! Get to it, man! There's no time to lose."

Carothers yanked off his hat and swiped a large palm over the top of his head. "Anthony! I might have known. Shove off and let us do our work."

"There's danger!"

"From a dead man? Hooey!"

Jim Anthony now stood in front of the crowd. Although his way was clear to join Carothers over the body, he made no move to draw nearer. "I'm telling you, get away from that corpse."

"And I'm telling you to shove off." Carothers rubbed at his eyes as if some foreign object was lodged in them.

Jim couldn't make Carothers understand that he possessed a seventh sense, perhaps from his ancestors, which detected things that are wrong, amiss. This extra sense, along with his nose and a vast wealth of medical knowledge had shown him deadly danger.

He turned to the crowd at his back and raised his arms expansively. "You've all had quite a shock I'm sure. My hotel is one block that way. The Waldorf-Anthony." He gestured with one muscular finger over the heads of the crowd. "As of now, we are offering complimentary dinners and open bar. For everyone here."

The effect this news had on the milling crowd was instantaneous. They broke and ran from the entrance of Mollari's. In seconds, Anthony stood alone, facing Carothers whose itchy eyes seemed to be giving him considerable discomfort. Jim observed him closely.

"How long have you been standing over the body?"

"We just got here."

"Then it may not be too late. Get away from there, you fool!"

The constable next to Carothers rubbed at his eyes and coughed. Jim noticed that many of the other constables were also rubbing at their eyes. Carothers cleared his suddenly dry throat and glared at Jim. He opened his mouth to speak but a spreading liquid suddenly began oozing out from beneath Woolcott's body. Jim saw this and his eyes bulged. With no one around to hear except trained police officers, he gave vent to what his senses had revealed to him upon his arrival.

"It's gas, Carothers. Mustard gas!"

The words froze the blood of the policemen. Many had been through the Great War and those two words: mustard gas, were enough to summon a plague of horrors to their terrified brains.

The puddle oozing out of Woolcott's cracked and blistered skin began to vaporize when it came in contact with the air. And the rising cloud was between the men and the exit.

Jim Anthony was a blur of movement. In one fluid motion, he yanked his handkerchief out of his pocket and lunged dangerously close to the spreading cloud and snatched a bottle off a drink cart near the entrance. He soaked the handkerchief in the liquid and proceeded to tie the sodden cloth across his mouth and nose. All the while the cloud of horrible, lingering death inched higher and higher like a vaporous wall.

Jim tensed his mighty legs and leaped forward towards the roiling cloud of mustard gas. Once through the front door, he slammed it shut behind him. Then like an Olympic diver he dove gracefully over the still rising cloud, somersaulting smoothly to come to rest standing next to a terrified Carothers.

"Didn't you hear me?" Jim said his voice muffled by the handkerchief around the bottom half of his face. "All of you! It's mustard gas! Quick, out the back way. Get to Penthouse A! My lab is there. Hurry!"

He shoved and cursed the men who seemed to come alive at his touch. They scattered like rabbits from the body. Jim, meanwhile, dashed about the restaurant making sure all the windows were closed. His burning curiosity urged him to examine the body for clues, but there was no telling how much gas the policemen had been exposed to. His first duty was to them. He retreated through the rear entrance after a final look around to make sure everyone was clear. He used his immense strength to haul a dumpster in front of the door.

Jim came out of the alley to find Tom Gentry preparing to enter Mollari's by way of the front door. "Tom!" he bawled. "Come away from there!"

"Golly, Jim! What the Sam Hill is going on? There're crowds of people storming the hotel with a bunch of scared silly coppers on their heels."

"A man has been killed by mustard gas. Carothers and his cronies have been exposed. The gas is trapped inside the building. As for the pedestrians, I had to get them clear and free chow and beers seemed to best way to do it. Stand guard here,

Tom, and stop anyone who tries to enter. Shoot them if necessary but keep that door closed. If the gas escapes, we could have dozens of people dead."

"You can count on me." With this Tom moved a good distance from the door, put his fists on his hips and his head on a swivel, his eyes missed nothing.

Jim Anthony sprinted back to the hotel.

Chapter 4

The incident at Mollari's kept Jim busy well into the night. With more than a dozen police officers to treat, and a compelling mystery to solve, he wanted the men handled with alacrity so he sent for Doctor Holman, the house doctor, to aid his work. Starting with Carothers, who seemed to be the worst for wear amongst the afflicted, Jim administered Peroxy acids. Sped by a catalyst, these went to work in seconds to negate the corrosive effects of the gas.

Mustard gas forms hydrochloric acid when it comes in contact with moisture and the human body, comprised mostly of water, provides the gas ample moisture to work with. Burns to the skin were simple enough to treat, but internal damage to the lungs and respiratory system was difficult to determine even though Penthouse A housed one of the best equipped, most advanced medical labs in existence. Jim performed the tests with superhuman expediency but the procedures were time consuming regardless.

Finally, when only minor cases remained, Jim felt comfortable handing the ball to Holman. Wiping his hands on a huck towel, he stepped from the lab and found Dawkins hunched over a radio in the living quarters. "Anything?"

"First h'off, Mephito wanted you to know that 'e gave Miss Colquitt somethin' to make 'er sleep. As for the radio, things h'are startin' to drip h'in now," Dawkins said, coming to his feet, his thin, wrinkled face awash in the glow from the radio.

Jim had instructed Dawkins to issue the Anthony Call. This was a general alarm and inquiry to the myriad of Anthony's helpers not only in the city but all over the world. The man sitting next to you on the trolley or at the lunch counter... these could be amongst Jim's army of helpers. Also doctors, scientists, politicians and street sweepers – they all made up a vast network of information gatherers dedicated to Jim Anthony's battle against crime.

"What have they dug up so far?" Jim asked.

"Well, ol' Woolcott's not the first h'industrialist to meet 'is h'end this way. H'I've put them h'on finding h'out who h'is behind h'it."

"I can save you the trouble." This from Carothers demonstrating considerable pluck in hauling himself out of a sick bed to join them in the living room.

"You know something," Jim breathed. "Let's have it."

Carothers leaned against the radio table and fought for breath. "The Crimson Scorpion is behind these ghastly murders," he explained. "He's killed three others that we know of."

"How was it done?"

"The same as Woolcott back there. Poison at any rate."

"The others couldn't have been killed by mustard gas," Anthony stated. "You wouldn't have been fool enough to stand so close to Woolcott's body if that were the case."

"You're right there. In the case of Mr. Daniel Dickson Bellamy, he was aboard ship and the body was stowed away until they made port. So if gas were used, there was no trace of it by the time the doctors got to him. The same goes for Maxwell Faust who the Scorpion cut down on his secluded ranch. As for the last victim, before Woolcott that is, Humphrey J. Stackpole, the Scorpion got him on a busy New York street. Just like Woolcott. Our lab people have not yet finished their examination. I'll lay odds on what they find."

"H'If what you say h'is true," Dawkins began, "h'it seems this Crimson Scorpion 'as been content, so far, to strikin' from the shadows. Why was Woolcott slain h'in so heinous h'and public h'a manner?"

Before Carothers could answer, Jim Anthony spoke.

"To be made example of. Woolcott was in a public place, the same as Stackpole, and no doubt could have been killed quietly. The more horrific Woolcott's death, the more sheer terror would be generated. The Crimson Scorpion must be secure in his base of operations to expose himself in this way. We have to act fast if we're to get him. Do the police know anything about him?"

Carothers shook his weary head. "Only that his intended victims receive a telegram shortly before they are murdered. To receive this telegram means certain death. I can't begin to tell you how much pressure is being brought to bear on the department. We're under the gun on this one. The city's rich and powerful live in abject terror of the Crimson Scorpion." He struggled to his feet, tugged his uniform into place. "But we don't need your help, Anthony. You saved me from a rough end and I felt I owed you. That's why I told you the Crimson Scorpion is behind the murders. That's as far as that goes though. Leave him to us."

"What became of their respective fortunes?" Jim asked. His voice low, eyes distant. "The other men all controlled industries essential to the war effort. What became of these enterprises?"

"Snapped up. Absorbed."

Jim Anthony said. "Maybe someone is trying to cripple arms production."

"Look, we've already dug into that. Each of the murdered men's industrial empires was acquired by a different conglomerate. And all of the factories have immediately doubled production and, in one case, even tripled production. They've become shining examples of war production. There's nothing to what you're saying."

Jim stared straight ahead for a moment, his super brain churning efficiently, then he leapt up and sent Dawkins into the lab for something. As Dawkins entered the lab, Jim thought he saw a shadow move behind the door. "I'm going to have a look at the body."

"I told you to leave it alone."

"You're welcome to come along."

"I'm in no condition for adventuring. My mind works though so I'll send my men to do my adventuring for me." He hobbled to the phone and verbally abused the operator until he was connected with police headquarters. He barked orders, then paused to hold the line a moment. "I'll have none of your interference, Anthony. Mark my words." His tone softened a fraction. "Say, what was that trick with your handkerchief? You tied it around your face. I could barely see from the gas, but it looked as if you'd wet it first with something."

"Bicarbonate of soda." Jim noticed the shadow again as Dawkins returned carrying a square case. There was a lot of noise coming from the lab as the injured men moved about, talking excitedly about the catastrophe they had narrowly avoided. The shadow withdrew from behind the door.

Carothers growled. "Can't you answer a simple question?"

"I answered your question."

Carothers was unaware that bicarbonate of soda was an effective defense against mustard gas when employed in the way Jim Anthony had used it. The protection was temporary but effective. "Stay away from Mollari's!" He bellowed as he turned his attention back to the telephone. But his reserves of strength seemed to fade. He barely spoke two words before slumping into the chair by the telephone. He drifted into a morphine-induced sleep, cradling the telephone receiver against his cheek.

Jim threw on his coat. The Crimson Scorpion had stirred his insatiable curiosity and he had to find out what was behind these attacks on the world's rich and powerful. Why would the Crimson Scorpion murder these men, then allow their war factories to increase productivity?

The doorbell chimed.

Dawkins saw to it and returned bearing a yellow envelope.

"It's a telegram," he said, stating the obvious.

Jim Anthony and Dawkins exchanged meaningful looks as the telegram was handed over.

Anthony slid a thick finger under the flap and extracted the missive. He read it quickly, handed it to Dawkins and, with case in hand, walked boldly from the room.

Dawkins read:

To: James Anthony
Death walks behind you.

Chapter 5

Jim spotted Tom Gentry's hulking, battered form outside the restaurant scowling at everyone who came within spitting distance of the place. "Seen anything fishy?" Jim asked.

"I chased off a couple of gawkers, but there's not been a soul the last few minutes," Gentry replied. The fog was lifting slowly but visibility was still greatly reduced.

Jim set the case down on the wet pavement. He snapped open the latch on the case and a corresponding crack sounded as if from far off. But this was no echo. The case spun out of Jim's hands.

"Someone's taking pot shots at us!" Tom bellowed.

Jim and Tom moved like one man as they dashed towards the restaurant. Jim had backtracked the bullet's trajectory and knew the shot had come from the alley beside Mollari's. He indicated this to Tom and they took up positions like sentries at either side of the alley mouth. A hail of bullets greeted this action, pummeling the walls behind which they took cover. Anthony darted his head around for a look at their attackers. In a split second he took in the scene and ducked safely behind the wall as clouds of brick dust erupted from the impact of hot lead. What Jim saw spurred him into immediate action.

"Well, Jim, do we rush 'em or creep around back?" Tom asked, a predatory gleam in his eye. This fevered blood lust transformed itself into a look of wide-eyed surprise as he turned to see Jim Anthony running away from the alley as fast as his feet could carry him. Tom didn't know what to make of this.

Jim ran with every iota of speed within his powerful legs back to the hotel. Not from fear or cowardice, but, rather, with deadly purpose.

Ambulances were pulling in here and there under the marquee in front of the hotel, their sirens growling down, lights flashing. Dr. Holman had followed Jim's instructions to move the exposed police officers to hospital to be sure there were no lasting side-affects from the gas. But the loading had not yet begun. A fact Anthony absorbed with some relief. The crowds lined up outside the hotel's restaurant and bar for free food and drink wrecked havoc with the ambulance attendants who could not get through to the entrance.

Jim skirted the milling crowd and dove into his private elevator. The specially designed car catapulted him up to Penthouse A.

Chapter 6

When the elevator doors parted Jim Anthony was met with a scene similar to the one he had just left downstairs. A crowd of swaying, leaning policemen were pressing towards the elevator. In the rear, Dr. Holman hollered for order but his reedy voice was lost in the cacophony of voices. Directly in front of Jim, facing the crowd, a frazzled floor clerk tried to keep the crowd back but the open elevator doors had galvanized the men into action and they pressed forward, an unstoppable wave that swept the hall clerk towards Jim who reached out a strong hand and steadied her from behind.

"Get ahold of yourselves!" Jim said. "You are in no danger. The hospital is just a precautionary measure. Shut up all of you. I'm not going to tell you again."

Any other man would have had to scream this fact repeatedly at the top of his lungs to be heard, but Jim spoke in a firm half-shout. His voice carried to the back row. The group gradually stilled and stood facing him expectantly.

"We will have you downstairs in a moment. Now, four or five at a time. Line up!"

Jim stepped out of the car to allow the first group to enter. His gaze bore into each

"To James Anthony— Death walks behind you."

face as they passed. Then his eyes locked on the face he sought. This officer, the third member of the first group, seemed to be in more haste than the others. His nervous eyes stabbed slyly left and right as he pressed forward. Anthony made as if to ignore the man until he passed by directly in front of the great adventurer. Then Jim lunged forward and clamped a vise-like hand onto the policemen's arm. The man yelped in surprise and tried to pull free but he would have the same measure of success trying to extricate himself from steel bear trap. He swung a wild fist at Jim who ducked, then drove a fist like a piledriver to the man's chin. The man crumpled instantly, dazed. The commotion drew the attention of Carothers who appeared all the better for his little nap.

"Here, now," he said coming to stand before Jim. "I'll not have you batting my men about. What's the meaning of this?"

"This man is a spy," Jim Anthony said, still holding the woozy officer. "He is an agent of the Crimson Scorpion."

"That's officer Reynolds," Carothers said. "My right hand man for the last three months. You've flipped, Anthony."

"Have I? We'll see."

In less than two minutes, the corridor was clear except for Jim, Carothers, and the man identified as Reynolds. Dr. Holman had volunteered to go along with the men to the hospital. Jim threw his burden over one shoulder and headed into his headquarters.

"You're keeping a good man from receiving hospital care, Anthony," Carothers spat as he followed the adventurer into Penthouse A. "Explain yourself. And make it good or I'll run you in. In fact I may run you in regardless."

Jim dumped the man onto a sofa, then stood between Reynolds and the door.

"Right now, the Crimson Scorpion's men are shooting up the neighborhood and at Tom. And I know why."

The revelation that gun play was going on along the streets of his city propelled Carothers to the window but the fog was still too thick this high up to see the street. Carothers smacked the glass in frustration. "Damn it!" He turned and glared at Jim. "I told you to steer clear of Mollari's. Now look what you've done!"

"It's not my doing. Ask Reynolds here."

"I got nothing to say to you or anyone!" Reynolds seethed.

"Quite right, my man." Carothers nodded before confronting Anthony. "Since when do police officers answer to you, you big muckety muck?"

"When they're not police officers."

"Enough of your blasted riddles."

"All right," Jim said. "I'll spell it out for you. When we spoke earlier I noticed someone hovering just inside the lab door, which was open. I saw the shadow again when I sent Dawkins for the case. Just now, the man made sure he was in the first group going down. His eyes gave him away."

Carothers sneered. "Sounds airtight." He turned to Reynolds and said, sarcastically, "He's got you dead to rights – the charge, loitering."

"Moments ago," Jim continued, unfazed by the noise coming from Carothers.

"Agents of the Crimson Scorpion shot at me and Tom from the alley adjacent to Mollari's. This was a covering move. I caught a glimpse of what they were up to. They were loading Woolcott's body into a truck."

"And what does that have to do with Reynolds?"

"The men were wearing protective suits against the mustard gas."

"Oh, I see. Well, that clears things up. Come along Reynolds, it's the chair for you."

"The men were wearing the same type of suit that was in the case I sent Dawkins into the lab to get."

"What of it?"

"Without a suit of this type, no one can get near the body. The restaurant is locked up tight. I did this myself. Tom is stationed outside. There was no chance of me, or anyone examining the body thus there was no immediate danger to the Crimson Scorpion or his men. Then this man hears me say I'm going to conduct an examination and sees Dawkins retrieve protective gear against the gas. We arrive at Mollari's to find hoodlums hastily spiriting the body away. As the body was perfectly safe where it was, how could the Crimson Scorpion have known I had the means to examine the corpse and that I was heading to the restaurant to do so?"

"That's not much to go on," Carothers said, rubbing his chin thoughtfully.

"It's plenty," Jim countered. "Reynolds eavesdropped on our conversation. A conversation which took place after several hours spent here treating the injured. Hours in which the Crimson Scorpion could have removed Woolcott's body with little opposition as only Tom was watching the place. Yet, for hours, they did nothing. Because they knew the body was off limits. That is, until they got word that I was heading there with protective clothing. Then suddenly they are compelled to remove the body."

"Maybe they thought the gas had dissipated by this time. Maybe they had to wait all those hours," Carothers said.

"The men I saw were wearing protective gear. The gas had not dissipated."

Carothers slowly digested what had been said. His look of disdain transformed to one of fury and he turned his inflamed eyes to Reynolds.

"Have anything to say, you rat!"

Reynolds rose up off the couch and made to rush past Anthony who shoved him backwards with considerable force.

"That settles it," Carothers fumed. "Your all washed up, Reynolds. Just wait 'til we get back to the station. You'll spill all you know about the Crimson Scorpion and do it gladly."

"There's a faster way," Jim Anthony said. "My brain message machine will get us all the information we need."

"If you think that infernal contraption will work, I'm game. But he's still going downtown afterwards."

Jim made as if to lay hands on Reynolds. The frantic officer made one last dash for freedom, slipping past Jim and smack into the arms of Tom who was returning at that same moment. Reynolds fought like a wild man, but Tom held him firmly.

"Lieutenant!" he cried. "You can't let them hook me up to that doohickey of his. You can't! Look, I took money to rat on you guys, I admit it. I slipped out of the lab and telephoned from the living room after Anthony and his men left. I admit everything. But it was wrong. I made a mistake. I know that now. Don't let them hook me up to that brain whatsit of his."

"If you're willing to talk," Jim said calmly, "then start saying the things we want to hear and maybe the brain message machine won't be necessary."

"All right, all right." Reynolds ceased struggling against Tom and slumped. Gentry still retained a firm grip in case the man was playing possum.

"You heard the man," Tom said, shaking Reynolds like a rag doll. "Spill!"

"The Crimson Scorpion has a hideout down at the waterfront. I was there once. It's his main base of operations. I tell ya, he must be there right now. It's an abandoned pier put aside for the war effort but the Navy hasn't gotten around to fixing the place."

"Come on, what else ya got?" Gentry shook Reynolds again.

"That's all, I swear. Get to that pier. But you better be armed for bear. There're gunsels all over the joint."

Jim nodded and Tom frog-walked Reynolds back to the sofa and threw him on it. Carothers, meanwhile, had steamed towards the telephone and was placing a call. While the operator transferred him, he turned and saw Jim whispering to Gentry and Dawkins who had joined them.

"Don't you go getting any funny ideas, Anthony," Carothers cautioned. "This is a police matter."

But Jim and Tom were already heading for the door. Dawkins went to guard Reynolds. Carothers got his connection and found himself caught between the telephone and the exiting adventurers.

"Damn it!" he spat. "Every time I get on this telephone that blasted Anthony gives me the slip." He slammed down the receiver and tore out after them.

Chapter 7

The elevator dropped them at their secret underground garage in seconds. They erupted out of the car and sprinted to one of the waiting sedans. Jim Anthony had a fleet of such vehicles, all designed to his precise specifications. They piled in and Jim gunned the engine to life. The motor, also a Jim Anthony invention, could put to shame anything currently running out at Indianapolis. The sedan roared out into the quiet night streets, leaving Carothers far behind. Under Anthony's expert control, the automobile was aimed straight at the waterfront.

Despite the lack of traffic, it still took a good fifteen minutes to reach the address Reynolds had provided. They arrived to find an abandoned warehouse leaning precariously to one side as the waves crashed against the pier upon which the building squatted.

"Golly, we're too late," Tom announced, slapping his hat against his leg.

Jim cursed hotly. "We were lied to. This is a diversion!"

They dove back into the sedan and Tom, as per Jim's direction, got behind the wheel and had the automobile rocketing back downtown. Jim did not know why they had been diverted from their headquarters, but suspected that it had something to do with the fact that Mephito and Delores had only Dawkins there as protection.

As they pulled up to the hotel, Jim dove out of the car. The graceful fluidity and ease of his movements belied the fact that the sedan was roaring up the street at better than forty miles per hour! An ordinary man would have been severely injured attempting a leap such as Jim Anthony had made. The Comanche giant launched himself through the front doors of the building, which housed their headquarters. Tom was close behind. They piled back into Anthony's private elevator and were catapulted up to Penthouse A.

The elevator doors parted. Jim streaked through the opening. Gun at the ready, Tom joined him at the door to their headquarters.

Muffled sounds could be heard coming from the other side of the door.

The door was locked but tendons like steel cables flexed in Jim's massive forearm and he thrust the door open.

They dived in.

And stopped dead.

They'd been expecting the Crimson Scorpion to be making his move out in the open at last. Instead they were met by a man, gun clenched in his fist and pointing right at them. Two men with pistols were with him.

Gentry bellowed and raised his gun.

"Try it," the man, whose name was Zimmer, spat, "if you want to get pinged like this sap." He pointed at Reynolds sprawled form with an oozing red hole in his forehead. Dawkins was tied up and squirming on the sofa. "Now drop the rod."

Tom reluctantly did so. He growled his displeasure. "Stuck up in our own digs. How humiliatin' can you get?"

More at ease now, Zimmer said, "That's better." He turned and faced Anthony. "You got here pretty fast."

"If you mean that little diversion," Jim began, calmly. "Reynolds did a poor job of it. The warehouse was clearly empty. Any fool could see that. No need to waste time on a fruitless search so you and your henchmen could set up your ambush."

Zimmer started at this bold statement. His eyes narrowed shrewdly. "I heard you were good."

"Where are Mephito and Delores Colquitt?"

"Roped up back there." Zimmer indicated the laboratory behind him. "You'll join 'em both if you give me any trouble."

"What do you want?" Jim hissed.

"The Crimson Scorpion already has what he wants. I should burn you down right now just to keep you out of his master plan but the Scorpion has other ideas." He raised the gun menacingly. "But don't try me. I could get used to the idea of burning you down in a hurry. Give me a good reason and the Scorpion won't mind, I'm sure."

Zimmer crabbed his way to the desk and perched on a corner or it. The men with him fanned out, covering their quarry with the ugly snouts of their automatics.

"Get out of them duds you three," he ordered. "The Scorpion knows all about the fancy doodads Jim Anthony keeps tucked away in his clothes. Well, I'll have none of that! Come on, lose 'em! I ain't taking no chances."

They had no choice but to comply. Tom all but tore the clothes from his large form, his beady eyes shooting daggers at Zimmer. Jim casually removed his outer clothes and handed them over to the thug who leaned forward warily to retrieve them. Eventually the clothes were in a pile on the desk beside Zimmer. He poked at them briefly as if searching for the weapons.

"Now what, big mouth?" Gentry growled.

"Have a seat." Zimmer gestured with the pistol. "Over there!"

They took chairs that stood near the room's large window. Jim and Tom had their backs to the window. Everyone remained motionless. Only the steady creep of the rising sun across the room showed the passage of time.

Zimmer started to fidget.

"Ryan," he addressed one of the men, "go check on our other pigeons. If they give you any grief, let 'em have it."

"Yes, Boss."

While their jailors were thus occupied, Jim wagged his fingers mysteriously. Tom and Dawkins nodded slightly. What their captors didn't know what that Jim Anthony and his associates were experts in sign language and that Jim had used his fingers to shape words.

Ryan returned and the three thugs riveted their eyes on the captives.

"What are we waiting for?" Jim demanded. "Does the Scorpion have the guts to meet me face to face?"

"The Boss doesn't need to waste time on the likes of you." Next to Zimmer, the pile of clothes emitted a thin wisp of white vapor.

Jim made a sound like he was clearing his throat but in actuality it was another secret cue to his associates. "Then why keep us here?"

Ryan noticed the trail of vapor near Zimmer. "Zim, what the - " Suddenly he rose up on his toes. He pitched forward and fell headlong. His companion crumpled like a puppet with its strings cut. The automatic he held clattered to the floor.

Zimmer stared agape at the scene, then staggered off the desk and tried to raise his pistol. "I'll burn you down! I—!" The gun tumbled from his nerveless fingers and he slumped down on his face.

Jim, Tom and Dawkins remained motionless for thirty seconds, then released the breath they had been holding. Gentry dashed forward and collected the weapons from the fallen men and determined that they were out.

"They will be unconscious for several hours," Jim Anthony explained.

"Jim how -- " Tom asked as he bent to untie Dawkins.

"Something new I perfected our last trip to The Tepee. It's a gas," Jim went on, "which remains solid and inert at 98.6 degrees but reverts to active vapor below that temperature. 98.6 degrees is the basic human body temperature. I impregnated my clothes with it. Once I removed the garments they quickly lost my body heat and released the gas."

Gentry and Dawkins were not surprised by this explanation. They had given up trying to figure out how Anthony accomplished the things he did. Jim and Tom threw on their clothes. Jim went to check on Delores and Mephito.

"Stay away from the windows," he said cryptically.

He returned a moment later.

"Mephito and Delores are out but otherwise uninjured. I placed them out of sight from the windows."

"What's going on?" Tom asked.

Jim did not respond to this query. "We must move quickly," he announced instead.

"What about these birds?" Tom asked.

"Leave them for now. There's no other way. Come on!"

That's when things started happening.

Jim's keen hearing detected the sound of glass shattering. His mighty arm rocketed up and snatched ahold of Dawkins' jacket. Dawkins yelped as Jim yanked him roughly to the floor. A lance of yellow fire sliced the air where the manservant's head had been a moment before and blasted a small hole in the wall. Another hot spear of death impacted a little farther down the wall to where they crouched. These were followed by a deadly hail that puckered the walls.

Jim tossed Dawkins bodily, like a bale of hay, into the waiting arms of Tom who squatted at the threshold of the front door like a baseball catcher. The angle of the room shielded him from harm. Bullets continued to slam into the wall, gouging tiny black holes and exploding priceless sculptures and works of art. Jim, keeping below the level of the windows, scrabbled after the others.

Chapter 8

Jim ordered Dawkins to the floor clerk's desk and the telephone there. Then Jim and Tom tumbled into the elevator. A few anxious seconds passed while they waited for the car to complete its rapid descent. After what seemed like ages to the passengers, the elevator gently touched down. They flew from the car and hit the street running.

The scene outside was one of undisturbed routine. Men and women moved about on their early morning commute unaware of what was taking place above their heads. Jim glided to the police call box on the corner. From a pocket he drew a key and it turned in the lock. He yanked the telephone receiver from the cradle.

"All units in the vicinity, this is Jim Anthony speaking. There is an emergency situation in the south building directly across the street from this location. Surround the building immediately. See that no one leaves."

He replaced the telephone and started across the street.

A dozen policemen came boiling out of doorways, alleys and coffee shops. All raced in the same direction as Jim and his associates. Anthony offered a few terse words of explanation to a bewildered Tom.

"I suspected a trap back at the warehouse and decided to use the Crimson Scorpion's plan against him. It was his intention to place us near the windows so we'd be easy pickings for the snipers setting up in the building across the street."

"Why didn't they just drill us outright?" Tom asked.

"It was a double feint," Jim explained as they made their way across the street. "If they had tried to shoot us, we wore our bulletproof undergarments, and would have fought back for all we're worth. And there's a chance we'd have licked them. The way they played it, they had us sit with our attention on Zimmer and the gunmen while their associates drew a bead on us from the roof of this building. The original plan was for us to be shot as soon as we were taken prisoner, but their attempt to draw us away long enough for the riflemen to get ready failed. And so Zimmer made us sit and wait. If I had not guessed their move in detaining but not killing us, their plan would have worked. What's important is that we now know where the shots came from and have the building surrounded. There's no escape. They'll have to use the elevators and, with the help of these officers, we'll have every exit covered."

A distant bassy whup-whup sounded above the noise of the converging constabulary. It was inaudible to the others but Jim heard it, turned his powerful gaze upwards and spotted the autogyro descending to the roof of the building.

Tom craned his neck. Realization spread across his features. "Dang it all! They'll get away!" He squalled.

"Get up there, fast!" Jim Anthony yelled. "Defend yourself if you have to, but we need one of the snipers alive for questioning."

With that he was off like a streak around back of the building. Behind him he heard the roar of gunfire being unleashed on the autogyro by the policemen on the ground. If they could drive the gyro off…

One massive leap later, he hung from the ladder of the fire escape. Like an Olympic gymnast, he swung and contorted his body until his feet clanged on the metal grill of the walkway. His powerful legs pistoned him up the stairs and he was at the edge of the roof in seconds. Here he paused to survey the scene. The two snipers were watching the gyro. But the gunfire from the street was giving the pilot more than he could handle. He had no choice but to climb to safety and he did this despite the wild gesticulations of the snipers on the roof.

Jim made his move.

He vaulted up over the edge and, using the air vents as cover, made his way stealthily toward the huddled riflemen. Sliding free his belt, Jim unspooled the fine-spun, thread-like material the belt was comprised of. Unwound, this material had the tensile strength of half-inch manila rope. The metal ball that served as a belt buckle dangled at his feet. He stood next to a pile of loose bricks left by workmen repairing the chimney. Jim picked one up and snapped it effortlessly in half.

Clutching the bolo in one mighty fist, he launched the half a brick directly at one of the assassins. It plowed into his side with terrific force. The man's eyes and mouth gawped. The rifle clattered from his hands and he collapsed into a ball of agony on the gravel.

"...Jim yanked him roughly to the floor."

While all this was going on, Jim had twirled the bolo over his head and let it fly at the other gunsel. It whistled through the air and, with the metal ball as a counterweight, it struck and coiled around the man's body like a boa constrictor, strangling off all movement. The man's rifle discharged, sending a bullet whizzing past Anthony's ear, but the man was immobilized, struggling like a hooked fish.

The hail of bullets from below suddenly ceased and the pilot of the autogyro dropped the craft down close to the rear end of the building. The gyro did not touch down as the pilot had seen Jim in action and did not want to get too close until his comrades had had an opportunity to eliminate their foe.

Thanks to Anthony's quick action, this was no longer possible. The injured rifleman, seeing his hog-tied companion, decided to give up the fight. He hobbled toward the hovering gyro as fast as his battered side would allow. Well aware of what the man intended to do, Jim forgot the helpless assassin and sprinted towards the fleeing man. Under normal circumstances, Jim Anthony would have easily won, but the gunman was much closer and made it to the edge of the roof off which hovered the gyro.

"Don't do it, man!" he shouted. "You'll never make it!"

Possessed by terror of what his employer would do to him if he fell into enemy hands, the man disregarded the warning and leapt feebly towards the autogyro. His outstretched hands missed the landing stanchion by more than twelve inches. With an anguished bellow, he fell from sight. Jim reached the roof in time to see the man's lifeless body sprawled in the alley below, a puddle of red oozing out from beneath it.

The pilot had seen enough. The machine's engine whined and the craft was hurled up into the morning sky, dwindling into the rising sun.

Jim turned without a second glance and went to the incapacitated prisoner. Tom burst onto the roof and, seeing Jim apparently alive and well, went to join him over the prisoner.

"Is that the lot of them?" Tom asked.

"No. One fell to his death." Jim said, scooping up the prisoner and tossing him over one shoulder. "We need answers, Tom. Let's get back to headquarters. There's not a moment to lose. Once the Crimson Scorpion learns his plan to eliminate us has failed, he'll take more certain and direct action."

Back on the street, they waded through the gathering throng of policemen. Aside from Carothers's vendetta against Jim Anthony, the Comanche giant had a generally good rapport with the force. Many the villain now resided in jail cells thanks to Jim's efforts and the men walking the beat were appreciative of this even if their superiors were not. Thus Jim and Tom were given free passage back into his headquarters. Jim went scudding through the crowd and back to the doors of the Hotel Waldorf-Anthony. They whipped back up in silence but Tom broke the silence when they entered their headquarters.

"Golly!" he roared.

There was no sign of the unconscious men. A quick survey of the rooms revealed Mephito laying face down in a pool of blood in the lab, his bag of shaman sticks kicked about. Dawkins lay in a heap on the living room floor, breathing raggedly next to Reynolds's corpse.

But of the others there was no trace. Zimmer and the gunmen were gone. And so was Delores!

Chapter 9

With Delores Colquitt in the hands of The Crimson Scorpion, Gentry and Dawkins expected Jim to explode into action. What manner of action they could not agree on, but they were sure it would be swift and decisive. What they did not expect, however, was for Jim to do nothing. For that is precisely what he appeared to do. It's not fair to say that he had no reaction at all. Actually his heart and mind were aflame with anxiety over his betrothed and a raging desire for revenge. However, upon discovering her abduction, and ascertaining that Mephito still breathed, he had handed the bound gunman to Tom, strode boldly into his lab and locked the door. There he remained for three hours.

The telephones jangled off the hook with calls from Jim's informants. Gentry and Dawkins, at first, paused in their ministrations to Mephito – rattled but not seriously injured – to field the calls, but no concrete leads came in. Their repeated banging on the lab door yielded no results and they resigned themselves to the fact that Jim would come out when he was good and ready and not a moment sooner.

Tom was drowsing in the living room later that morning while Dawkins prepared breakfast. Exhausted yet restless, Tom stood up to adjust his clothing, which had become twisted with his edgy fidgeting on the sofa. After pawing and yanking at the fabric, he turned to bat at the pillows of his makeshift bed, and there stood Jim Anthony behind the sofa, one hand on the lab door. Tom gasped in surprise. For Jim seemed to have aged fifteen years in the last three hours. No doubt from agonizing over the whereabouts of Delores Colquitt, Tom mused. The skin sheathing Jim's powerful muscles appeared pale, tight, somewhat parchment like with a sickly sheen to it. The flesh pulled taut around his skull giving him a skeletal appearance.

"Damn me, Jim!" Tom blurted, stunned by the wasted apparition before him.

"Bring the prisoner," was all Jim Anthony said by way of reply.

Gentry did so, shoving and cuffing the bound man forward to stand before Anthony.

"Are you sure you're up to it, Jim?" Tom asked. "You look like hell. I'm sure Delores is all right. That gal can take care of her—"

"What is your name?" Jim hissed at the captive rifleman.

The man drew himself up and glared at Anthony.

"It's Eddie. Eddie Dexter. Those who know what's good for 'em call me the Edge."

"I'll edge you right out that window if you don't mind your lip." Tom shoved Dexter hard to drive his point home.

"Watch it, you gorilla! I'm tight with the Scorpion. I give the word and you go toes up. Get me?"

"You will tell me where to find the Crimson Scorpion," Jim said in a half-mumble.

The skin around his lips appeared taught, restricting his speech.

"The hell I will!" Dexter spat. "I'll spell it out for you. You can't beat the Scorpion. No one can. So don't waste your time trying."

"If that's the case, then why won't you tell me where he is?"

"Because you'll slow things down, gum up the works if the Scorpion has to waste time mopping the floor with you. I stand to make a pile when all's said and done. I don't want nothin' slowing things up any."

"I see." Jim nodded. His fists were clenched so tightly that the knuckles turned white. "The Crimson Scorpion is afraid."

"The Scorpion fears no man!" Dexter tugged and writhed his hands meticulously against the rope binding his wrists.

"Yet you won't tell me where he is."

"That's right. And nothing will drag it out of me either."

Jim turned to Tom. "I've had enough of this. We'll use the brain message machine. Bring him."

"What's he talking about?" Dexter asked, his head swiveling back to face Tom.

"I'll state it plain for you, friend," Gentry said. "He means we'll get all the answers we need out of you with the brain message machine he invented. It's foolproof. You'll sing like a bluebird and the best part is there's nothing you can do to stop it."

Dexter began to sweat under Tom's taunts. He continued to slide and grip his hands together furiously.

"Jim?" Tom asked as he propelled Dexter towards the lab. "Doesn't the sap have to be sleeping for your invention to work?"

Dexter increased his deliberate hand rubbing until suddenly he was free. He shoved at Tom, grappled with him for an instant, then pulled free and dashed to the door.

He took two steps before crumpling from a precise judo chop to the back of the neck from Anthony.

"You're right, Tom," Jim said. "The subject must be asleep. But unconscious will do as well."

They carried Dexter to the lab. Jim pushed aside a pile of debris left over from his treatment of the afflicted officers and unceremoniously dumped the gunman down on an examination couch. Under the harsh lights of the lab, Jim Anthony looked even more ghostly and pale and Tom worried about his friend as Jim prepared the brain message machine for use.

The machine consisted of two components the first of which was a set of electrodes, which were placed at the subject's temples. The rest of the apparatus took the form of a radio-like box to which a graph was attached. A stylus carried a green ink line over the graph. Jim cleaned Dexter's temples with alcohol swabs, then affixed the electrodes. He switched on the radio-like box. The box made no noise. The electron tubes inside glowed faintly.

Softy, yet enunciating every word, Jim began, "What – is – your name? Think! Think!"

Jim's eyes moved to the stylus on the graph. There was no writing on the paper.

Rather the stylus scratched a single, saw-toothed, zigzag line across the scrolling paper. To the casual observer, the line meant nothing, but thanks to exhaustive experimentation on Anthony's part, each tiny green peak on the graph represented a letter of the alphabet. For he had invented a machine that actually inscribed the sleeping thoughts of any person.

Reading the peaks, Jim learned that the man's real name was Theodore Dietrich. The German surname came as no surprise to Anthony as the graph had spelled out Dexter's reply in German, which Jim had easily translated. This information, unfortunately, did not help their current situation beyond demonstrating that the machine was in good working order. The rifleman would not have changed his name to Eddie Dexter and suppressed his German heritage if he wanted these things known.

"I tell ya this thing still gives me the creeps," Tom admitted, then moved away from the machine to stand near the door.

"Who – is – the Crimson Scorpion?" Jim continued in a breathless, precise whisper.

The graph spelled out the name Ulrich Vankessel.

Anthony searched his capacious memory. Ulrich Vankessel was of German descent despite the Dutch family name. The Vankessel family controlled a vast empire of incalculable wealth. But Ulrich had been presumed killed in the Great War. Jim asked Dietrich why Vankessel had assumed the identity of the Crimson Scorpion but to this query he received no answer. Clearly the assassin did not know the answer.

"Where -- is -- Ulrich Vankessel?"

Once again Jim's gaze flicked to the graph. The answer spelled Ajax Petroleum. This was a petrochemical company in New Jersey, one of the largest producers of oil, gas and rubber crucial to the war effort. This was a company that had belonged to Daniel Dickson Bellamy, the first industrialist to fall to the Scorpion.

"Why – is the – Crimson Scorpion – killing – innocent – men?"

The graph began its zigzag rhythm. Jim leaned forward expectantly in the hope of learning what was behind the murders. His keen eye following the peaks on the paper, he spelled out BOO –

Then a soft crackling sound seemed to come from the man's head -- from directly under the electrodes! Jim Anthony's seventh sense kicked in, warning him of immediate, terrible danger.

"Tom!" he shouted. "The door! Open it!"

He was up in flash. Jim shoved Tom out, then followed his friend. This action took mere seconds. But these scant seconds were barely sufficient for just as the door banged shut, there was an explosion in the lab that shook the whole floor.

"What the devil!" Tom ejaculated as he fought to keep his balance.

Jim, feet wide apart, swayed slightly but did not lose his footing. "It was the Crimson Scorpion," he explained. "Just before the explosion, I detected a low sizzling noise coming from beneath the electrodes on Dexter's temples. This was a chemical reaction with the alcohol I used to sterilize the area. The chemical reaction produced the explosion. The Scorpion is a master chemist, that much is certain."

Tom asked. "How could the Crimson Scorpion know about your brain message machine?"

"Leading scientists of today were here just two weeks ago to study the machine. It has been written up in scientific journals. With the war on, there has been talk of using it as an interrogation tool."

"But the damn thing blew up!" Tom said.

Jim tapped his temple and smiled, grimly. "The plans are right here. I can build a replacement. What matters now is that we get to the Crimson Scorpion. He is at Ajax Petroleum in New Jersey. And that's where he'll be keeping Delores."

"Then we've got 'em," Tom said. "By golly! What are we waiting for?"

Chapter 10

entry had the sedan roaring through the morning light, heading west. Dawkins remained behind after receiving specific instructions from Jim. Tom still worried about Jim's state of mind. He'd hoped that a return to action would have returned his friend's fire, but Jim still seemed shrunken, shriveled and this preyed on Tom's mind. But this did not concern Jim Anthony. He needed to reach Gibbons, the managing editor at the New York Star, which Jim owned. He powered up the portable two-way radio and put the call in to Gibbons' eleventh floor office.

"Jim!" Gibbons exclaimed. "It's good to hear from you."

"Likewise, Gib," Jim replied. "I need information."

"Shoot."

"You've been following the murders committed by a man calling himself the Crimson Scorpion."

"Yes, of course."

"Good. Now I heard from Carothers that the murdered men all had ties to wartime production and that all their assets were quickly absorbed by rival conglomerates."

"True. All true."

"In every case, these manufacturing concerns doubled productivity after they'd been acquired."

"Every one. There was some anxiety in the beginning, what with war production being vital right now. But those plants are really cooking."

"Carothers went on to say that one of the factories actually tripled productivity."

"Oh, yes, that's right. The Times did a feature on that while you were out of town."

"Which factory?"

"Ajax Petroleum," Gibbons answered. "That Times piece nearly buried us when it hit the stands. It was all anyone was talking about."

"Thanks, Gib."

"By the way, speaking of Carothers, he's been blasting my ear off trying to find you. If he calls again, what should I tell him?"

"Tell him he'll be hearing from me within the hour."

Jim switched off the two-way and returned the handset to the cradle.

"What's all this about where we're going?" Tom asked.

"Ajax tripled productivity, while the other factories only doubled theirs. And Ajax was the first property acquired when this mess began."

"Think it means something?"

"Maybe nothing. Maybe everything," Anthony replied cryptically.

They powered across the bridge into New Jersey and Tom pointed the sedan in the direction of Ajax. Assuming the Crimson Scorpion would be monitoring the roads, Jim directed Tom to take a roundabout route to the factory. As they lanced through a narrow stand of trees, they could see the soaring chimneys of Ajax in the distance.

"Pull over here," Jim said.

Gentry did so and Jim Anthony had the door open before the machine came to a full stop.

"You go on ahead, use the front entrance, make like a businessman eager to throw contracts their way. That'll get you past security. Get a tour of the place."

"What about you?"

"I'll find another way in. Get moving."

Jim watched the sedan until it disappeared around a bend in the road, then got moving himself. Sure-footed as a jungle cat, he called on the instincts and expertise of his Comanche ancestors to creep through the woods in the direction of Ajax. He encountered several trip wires as he made his approach, which would have snared any other man, but to Jim they were as plain as billboards and he easily avoided them.

At last, he found himself a mere fifty yards from the Ajax building. It was a long, squat structure with soaring smokestacks here and there along its length. The building appeared to be unguarded from the outside but that could be a deception. It seemed unlikely that the lair of the Crimson Scorpion could be approached so easily.

After burning every detail of the exterior of the plant in his mind, he retreated back into the shadow of the trees. He'd noticed an old air vent overgrown with vines. Making sure not to disturb the natural growth, lest the adjustment be noticed by any of the Scorpion's men, he applied his awesome strength to the rusted grate and it wrenched open with a muffled, rusty screech.

Jim dropped inside, holding the grate partially open over his head with one hand while he eased back the vines with the other. Once the plants covered the grate, he slid it all the way back into place and, with his back against one wall of the shaft and his legs thrust out against the opposite side, he inched his way down.

He hit bottom and the vent widened slightly and ran horizontally to where he'd entered. Hunched over, he raced along the length of the shaft in utter darkness. He relied on his forest sense to guide him and it revealed the wall of the factory in front of him before he collided with it. Usinig his hands, which seemed to have cunning eyes on each finger, he traced the surface of the wall and found the vent grill. This grill was unlocked and swung open with hardly a complaint.

Another shorter shaft ran into the complex. This shaft was lit faintly and Jim could see a third grill not too far ahead. Once past this he would be in the bowels of the plant. Thoughts of Delores and what she might be suffering at the hands of the Crimson Scorpion came to him here and, cursing, he covered the intervening space rapidly.

With the last grill back in place to cover his trail, he glided his way through the pipes and conduits running the length of the basement chamber. Scalding water dripped onto his back, jets of steam burst with malice into his face, but he soldiered on, his seven senses missing nothing. The pipes rattled and gurgled with manic intensity belying the extraordinary productivity recorded by the Times and mentioned by Carothers. He noticed two immense cylindrical glass tanks against one wall with thick metal pipes running out of them to disappear into the ceiling. The strange liquid in the tanks confirmed suspicions he had, but there was no time to investigate further. He had to find Delores!

He moved on. The narrow passage through the maze of pipes pointed in only one direction. His seventh sense told him all he needed to know about the passageway dead ahead, but there was no alternative.

He stepped boldly into the passageway.

A metal door suddenly clanged shut behind him. Some thirty feet from him, a second door stabbed down and banged shut before he could blink.

He was trapped!

"I have been monitoring your approach," a disembodied voice said from a speaker set into the corner made by the wall and roof behind him. "Allow me to commend you on your stealth. Of course it is all so much wasted effort."

The voice was a deep rumbling bass, the accent clearly German in origin.

It was the Crimson Scorpion who spoke!

"Where is Delores Colquitt, Vankessel?"

"Do not use that name!" the Scorpion hissed. "As for the girl, she is quite safe for the present. Speak that name again and her condition will change. And not for the better, I assure you."

Jim breathed a sigh of relief. The news of Delores eased a small corner of his mind and he could now focus wholly on the danger ahead. His blood, however, boiled at hearing the Scorpion say her name!

"I offer you a choice," the Scorpion went on. "Surrender now or I shall flood the chamber with poison gas. Which shall it be?"

This was really no choice at all as Jim well knew.

"All right, Scorpion. You have me. I surrender."

"Excellent!" the Scorpion crowed triumphantly. "There will be armed men waiting on the other side of the door. They all are wearing protective masks. One hint of resistance from you and I shall release the gas."

The door at the far end of the passageway opened and the men filed in, guns raised and aimed directly at his midsection. They took possession of Anthony who offered no resistance.

Chapter 11

They searched him roughly, yet clumsily, discovering the explosive cartridges Jim always carried, then took him through a labyrinth of corridors to a lavishly furnished room.

In the shadow of the dim room, seated at the expansive desk, sat a figure cloaked in darkness.

"Mr. Anthony, at last."

"What is it you want, Vankessel?"

"I told you never to speak that name!" The Scorpion's voice boomed from wall to wall in the room, echoing as if it issued from every corner.

Jim fixed the shrouded, seated figure with his stony gaze while the men put the cartridges on the desk for the Scorpion's inspection. "What is it you want?"

"My needs are very specific," the Scorpion said, calmly. "And do not require your cooperation. Your presence is sufficient. Bring them!"

A door on Jim Anthony's right opened and the guards thrust Tom and Delores into the room. Their hands were bound and a thin trickle of blood traced its way down Gentry's brow. One shoulder of Delores' dress hung down, revealing a creamy, alabaster shoulder and a portion of her brassiere. Seeing her betrothed, she made as if to run to Jim, but the guards held her back. Jim managed to conceal his relief at seeing Tom and Delores alive and well, relatively speaking.

"As for what I want, I am well on my way to achieving it. I shall see the Fatherland returned to its former glory!"

"Single-handedly you will bring this about?" Anthony jeered.

The Crimson Scorpion chuckled. "Ah, there we are in agreement. In the grand scheme of things, what is an individual life after all? Its worth is determined by the value the individual places on it."

Jim took a step towards Tom and Delores.

"In the last war," the Scorpion went on, warming to the topic, "I fought for the Fatherland, and would have gladly laid down my life for Germany. That is until the rumblings of surrender spread like pestilence through the ranks. The day the armistice was signed, I turned my back on Germany, I thought, forever. In my shame, I would surrender to the Americans, renounce my heritage and see to my own dreams and aspirations. It was a dismal, rainy twilight when I marched across no man's land to the American lines. I expected an enemy bullet at any moment, but it did not come. I soon learned why. A gas attack! There was no peace in this corner of the battlefield! As the gas erupted around me, and I felt its first hellish sting, the Heavens let loose a divine lightning bolt, which struck me at the same instant as the gas, fusing my body with the deadly poison, which can no longer harm me. My life was spared. I was transformed. But with some startling side effects!"

Anthony sensed the movement behind him and dodged faster than the eye could follow.

However the figure behind him lashed out with blinding speed, a tiny hot-dagger

"He was trapped!"

pinprick stabbed the skin on the inside of Jim's right wrist. The lights flared in the room as Jim performed a forward roll and came up facing his attacker. Before him stood the Crimson Scorpion! The room now bathed in stark light, Jim could see that it was a dummy seated at the desk – a decoy while the real villain crept up from behind.

Delores shrieked at the sight of the Scorpion and hid her eyes behind her bound hands. The others took in every lurid detail of their foe's appearance. Although concealed by a cape as black as night, there was more than enough of the Scorpion's horrid form to be seen. The hairless oblong head tapered to a hooked nose and bloodless lips. Piercing ebony eyes beneath a wrinkled, lowered brow, sucked in all light. The large hands and misshapen face were scarred, red and raw with obscene blotches the color of ketchup. The Crimson Scorpion was tall, gangly. Beneath the cape he wore a scarlet close-fitting coverall that revealed deceptive, sinewy strength and power.

He clutched a peculiar looking handgun in the mottled fist of his left hand. The gun consisted of an ovoid, tapered barrel with a short grip. He menaced Anthony with it, the poisoned, metal-capped fingers of his right hand raised and poised like so many claws to strike.

"That scratch you felt came from these," the Scorpion held up his right hand. "I could have used this I suppose." He brandished the gun. "But I wanted to fell the mighty Jim Anthony at close quarters. You should be feeling dizzy about now."

Jim scrutinized the scratch on his wrist. While he was looking at it, he suddenly swayed.

"Yes!" the Scorpion hissed. "You are feeling it. The gas is not fatal. Though when your breath dries up in your throat you might think it is."

Jim's eyes bulged as his hands went to his throat. He struggled for breath.

"Next will come paralysis. You will hear everything that transpires, but you will be unable to move."

Jim Anthony pitched forward awkwardly and rolled onto his back. His arms and legs went rigid, sticking straight out from his sprawled body in the middle of the floor. His eyes remained fixed on the ceiling.

The Crimson Scorpion went and stood over his vanquished opponent. He showed Jim the gun. "Impressive, isn't it?" he asked. "Within the hour, I leave for the Fatherland with the plans for this weapon. Plans I will turn over to the Reich upon my arrival. This, along with my poison gas formulas and the compact cartridges you so generously donated to the cause, Germany will be invincible. My work here is done. Almost."

He turned, his cape billowing around him, and barked at the guards. "Leave those two and ready the transport."

The men threw the captives forward. Tom and Delores fell to their knees.

The Crimson Scorpion once more regarded Anthony. "This weapon fires a poisonous dart. Oh, the dart is not lethal to the target, at least not right away, but it renders the target highly contagious. The virus is one of my own devising and there is no cure. I tested a minute dose of the virus mixed with mustard gas -- enough to kill one man -- on Woolcott and it is deadly. I had the body brought here to determine the effectiveness of the virus. I am going to inject you and your friends with the contagion mixed with my paralyzing formula. As you will be unable to speak or move when the authorities arrive, the contagion will spread to them while you lay helpless. By the time the paralysis wears off, the virus will be rampant in the city. An epidemic will result. And you will be the cause of it. My supply of the virus is limited here, but the Reich has promised me unlimited resources. There will be no stopping us this time!"

The Crimson Scorpion moved from Jim's prostrate form. "I shall infect your associates first so as to prolong your anguish. Do not worry, though, soon you, too, shall bear my invisible death mark."

"Damn it, Jim, we can't let this devil get away with it!" Gentry yelled. "Before they conked me, I saw the plant. They're spraying something queer on stuff before they crate 'em. Canteens, belts, helmets -- everything our boys in combat use! Guys in suits like the one you wanted to use back at the restaurant are doing the sprayin'. We've got to do something!" He saw the Scorpion coming towards him, gun raised. "Delores get behind me!"

As the Crimson Scorpion bore down on the helpless captives, their eyes widened saucer-like with fear and he relished it. As his scarred crooked finger applied pressure to the trigger, he noticed that the eyes of his terrified prisoners were no longer on him, but were fixed, rather, on something over his shoulder. Something behind him.

A hand like a vise clamped on the Scorpion's wrist. Numbing pain shot up his forearm and he dropped the gas gun but not before propelling a stream of mini-darts into the carpet at the feet of Tom and Delores.

The Crimson Scorpion whirled, claws poised to strike. Jim released the gun hand and leapt gracefully out of the way of the lethal swipe of the needle claws. The Crimson Scorpion, gradually realizing that Anthony had somehow shaken off the effect of his paralysis gas, hesitated for a startled instant before stooping to retrieve the pistol.

Tom chose that moment to strike. He clubbed his hands between the shoulder blades of the Scorpion, knocking him to one side. Gentry could not pick up the gun with his hands tied so he kicked it into the corner. The Scorpion flailed with his claws as he stumbled forward but did not fall. Jim had no angle to move in.

So instead he seized the moment to put a shoulder like a bowling ball into the door, which flew open under this assault. "Tom! Delores! Go! The police are on their way!"

The two, reluctant to leave Jim but resigned to the fact that there was no other course of action, scurried from the room. Anthony stood between them and the Scorpion.

"All right, Vankessel. Let's finish this!"

They came together like two charging tigers. Jim gripped the Scorpion's right hand and held the deadly claws at bay. He chopped viciously with his other hand, seeking the sensitive nerve clusters in his opponent's body. For his part, the Scorpion fended off this attack as he fought to free his clawed hand. He did not know how

Anthony had neutralized the gas, but, if he could free his hand for a fraction of a second, he would deliver a fatal dose from his poison-tipped claws and that would be the end of Jim Anthony.

Although the Scorpion was taller, Jim's considerable strength gave him leverage and he forced the Scorpion back. Vankessel, instead of resisting, suddenly gave way and the two tumbled over the desk, scattering the items atop it. Papers flew, the dummy broke apart, and the desk lamp fell to the floor a split-second before the Scorpion and Jim crashed down upon it.

The bulb of the lamp exploded with a mute pop. The two adversaries rolled around on the broken glass, which crunched beneath them. The sputtering lamp socket threw sparks over the strewn papers and flames licked up at them as they struggled. The Scorpion sat atop Anthony. Gathering his legs under him, Jim heaved the Scorpion over his head and sent him crashing into the wall.

Only slightly winded by this, the Scorpion nevertheless feigned weakness to catch Jim off guard. Eyes closed he slumped, then sprang forward, claws raised to deliver the killing blow.

Jim Anthony moved a fraction of a second faster.

He seized the sputtering lamp from the rising flames and jammed it forward to meet the oncoming metal claws of the Scorpion. The claws burrowed into the live socket. Sparks exploded outwards and the Scorpion's body jerked frantically. Jim instantly released the lamp and backed away. A jet of flame shot from the claws. The already mottled red skin of the Scorpion seemed to take on an even more livid hue. Smoke rose from his body and Jim could sense the heat coming from the man. With a spastic shake, the Crimson Scorpion was able to fling the lamp aside to clatter against the wall. Still smoking, eyes aflame, he turned and faced Anthony.

"Even in my weakened state I am more than a match for you. You have lost!"

Jim had retreated to the door. A sly grin tugged at one corner of his mouth for when he had seized the lamp from the fire he'd noticed something else in the fire. "Those explosive cartridges, which were to be your gift to the Reich, they are heat triggered."

"No!" The Crimson Scorpion's eyes went wide as he saw the flames closing in over the cartridges on the floor.

Jim darted to the safety of the hall. When the explosion erupted, the blast wave, trapped by the narrow hallway, knocked him off his feet. A gout of flame lanced out into the corridor, singeing his eyebrows.

In seconds it was over.

Jim Anthony stood, brushed himself off, then went to find the others.

Chapter 12

Jim found Tom and Delores in the entranceway, speaking with Carothers who shouted orders left and right. He hurried over.

"What in the devil have you done this time, Anthony?" Carothers roared.

"That explosion all but shook the place apart."

"The Crimson Scorpion is dead," Jim replied, calmly. "But there's still danger. There is poisonous gas here -- gas in the hands of individuals loyal to the Scorpion. You need to secure the plant. Did you get Dawkins's call and alert the Coast Guard?"

"Yes. We're not monkeys, you know."

"Did you shut down the other plants?"

"Yes, yes! Now, look, Anthony, maybe the Coast Guard and the Commissioner are willing to drag half of law enforcement into this on your word, but I'm not. I want answers!"

"It's really quite simple," Jim explained. "The Crimson Scorpion murdered those men in order to seize their assets."

"That's where you're wrong. Different corporations absorbed each empire. I told you we looked into that."

"Look again, you will find that they all belonged to Ulrich Vankessel, the Crimson Scorpion."

"But, Jim," Tom said. "Didn't Carothers here tell us that the munitions plants all doubled their productivity?"

"That was the key to it, Tommy boy. You saw it with your own eyes. That mist you saw them spraying on war materials before packing them – this was the deadly poison the Scorpion tried to use on us. The materials treated here would not touch human flesh again until they were in the hands of our soldiers on the battlefield. His aim was to spread contagion through the ranks. That was why Vankessel pushed the factories to increase production. Also, to do otherwise would arouse suspicion. If productivity went up, no one would investigate what was going on. Meanwhile our fighting men overseas were being issued silent, deadly booby-traps. Yes, Tom, that's what Dietrich was trying to say just before he succumbed to the trap laid for us by the Scorpion back at the lab. The weapons manufactured by these plants are all booby-trapped. That's why I told Dawkins, before heading here, to alert the Coast Guard and the police. The freighters carrying the deadly cargo must be intercepted."

"The Coast Guard got 'em" Carothers said, shaking his head at the enormity of the consequences had they not tipped to the plan. "We've cabled the Supply Corps overseas, they're recalling everything that got across from these factories."

"Then it's finally over," Delores sighed, clinging tightly to Anthony's massive arm.

"Not quite, honey," Jim said. "Vankessel said there was no cure for the poisons he'd created, but he had to be lying. If an accident occurred amongst his minions, it would spell his doom the same as it would for our soldiers. The cure is here and we have to find it."

"Leave that to me and my men," Carothers said. "You've done enough for today."

"If you need a hand, just whistle," Jim said to Carothers' back as the lieutenant strode away from him into the plant.

"Golly, Jim, it's all so fantastic," Tom said in wonderment. "Say, speaking of poison, how did you shake off that gas the Crimson Scorpion got you with? If it's as bad as you say…"

Jim Anthony reached across and appeared to peel a layer of skin from the back of his hand. Reaching up, he did the same for his face and neck, coming away with a sheer, transparent mask. The pinched, drawn aspect of Anthony's face Gentry had worried about earlier was instantly gone. He saw now what had altered Jim's features.

"Plasti-skin," Jim said. "I applied it after Delores was taken. The deaths of Woolcott and Stackpole, occurring in public places, told me that the Scorpion had to have a discreet way of striking. I thought a needle of some kind and I was partially right. Before facing him, I protected myself with the plasti-skin. When he thought he'd scratched me, I played along until his back was turned. The rest you know."

"The important thing is you're safe," Delores said. "I was scared to death back there."

"It'll be a lot scarier if our boys aren't given the tools and support they need to get the job done. We've all got to do our part this side of the pond."

And, with that, they left the factory and headed back to face whatever future challenges awaited them.

THE END

Writing "Death Walks Behind You"

Sitting down to write a Jim Anthony adventure was a daunting task because I had never heard of the character. I quickly learned that he was, perhaps, the most successful Doc Savage clone of the 40s and this intrigued me enough to want to write an Anthony story. Being steeped in the lore of the man of bronze, I felt this gave me a handle on the character and what constituted a Jim Anthony tale. However, for me, it is extremely important to honor the creators of the past and I simply did not feel comfortable writing an Anthony adventure without absorbing the tone, characterizations, gadgets, settings and nuances of the original pulp tales. I wanted to get it right. Not only for Jim Anthony fans picking up the story, but also out of respect for the original creators who strived to excel for little or no money at a demanding pace. Writing is not easy and anyone who claims it is probably does not do it very well. Jim shares similarities with Doc Savage but the differences far outweigh them. His eye for the ladies, hot temper and unwavering commitment to getting results by any means set Jim apart from his bronze counterpart. In one classic tale, he belts Tom Gentry unconscious when his dear friend disappoints him and this comes after he has fired everyone who works for him in a fit of rage. Yup, Jim is his own character and capturing this tone was the hardest part of crafting my tale. Whether I have succeeded in capturing the feel of a Jim Anthony adventure, only the reader can judge.

The genesis of the story came from, of all places, an AC/DC song. The tune in question: *"Evil Walks"* from the *For Those About To Rock* album. Listening to the song one afternoon while gently urging inspiration to raise its reluctant head, I was struck by some of the lyrics which ran: *"Black shadow hanging over your shoulder/ Black mark up against your name."* When these were followed by the line: *"There's black poison running through your veins/ evil walks behind you,"* the idea popped into my head to have Anthony confront a villain who uses poison as a weapon and strikes his victims from behind. Like a scorpion. Crimson, being a word used frequently in pulp fiction for its power, seemed the best way to describe my villain and the Crimson Scorpion was born. Tying the Scorpion's villainous plot to wartime production gave the story, I thought, a nostalgic ring that made it seem more of that era where the tale belongs after all. The original title of the story was "Evil Walks Behind You" but, seeing as the Scorpion sends this message to his victims before he strikes, it didn't seem right that he would refer to himself as evil. I toyed with "Death Stalks Behind You" but this seemed awkward so I settled on "Death Walks Behind You." Now all I had to do was write the story.

The writing of the tale was great fun. A lot of hard work, but fun hard work – if such a thing is possible. Pulp has its own unique voice with a flavor all its own. Like jazz, you know it when you hear it and this voice harkens one back to the 30s and

40s. Sadly the pulp voice is a lot like Latin in that very few people practice it these days. So, to write in this style, means to basically ignore the writing rules of today. Over the top flowery language, break neck pacing, heroes with almost super human abilities and a well-defined sense of right and wrong – this is pulp fiction to me. It is a distinct art form, difficult to do well. Writing pulp is also very liberating for the reason stated above: you get to throw out the rules! But you must do so under control, paring away lengthy descriptions so only action and tight plotting remain.

Pulp fiction served an important role during the Depression years. Its function, ultimately, was to distract the reader from the daily woes of little or no work or bread on the table. The aim was to sweep the reader away from these daily trials by not giving him or her a chance to breathe through non-stop action. And, poring over old sales records, it succeeded in doing this, giving the voice a hint of noble intent. I love the pulp voice and didn't know if I could write it. Until a group of dedicated Doc Savage fans banded together to do a collaborative novel to celebrate the 70th anniversary of the character. Each writer would contribute a chapter to the work, taking the story to untold heights of excitement. I got Chapter 7. As the chapters began piling up, and number 7 loomed, I was more than a little anxious about whether or not I could write in the pulp voice as I had never attempted to do so before. Finally when time came to sit down and do my part, I found the voice was just *there*. Because it liberates one from the writing rules of today, I just turned myself loose and the voice came naturally to me and I finished Chapter 7 in, for me, record time. Sadly the Doc collaborative novel fell through, but I was proud of my chapter, which is why you'll find that Doc chapter in *"Death Walks Behind You."* Rewritten as a Jim Anthony chapter of course. For those interested, it is Chapter 8. Since Doc Savage introduced me to the world of pulp just 7 years ago, it seemed fitting to insert a Doc chapter into my first pulp story. Hopefully the insertion has proceeded flawlessly and this is the first you're hearing of it.

The opportunity to write pulp for Airship 27/Cornerstone is, literally, a dream come true. After devouring 90 or so Doc stories and a handful of Shadow tales all washed down with generous servings of Max Brand, Edgar Rice Burroughs and the great hardboiled detective writers of the Golden Age like Mickey Spillane, John D. Macdonald and Cornell Woolrich, I ached to do this kind of writing but felt there was no market for it. So I had to put the desire aside in favor of more potentially commercial enterprises.

Now, thanks to Airship 27/Cornerstone, I'm a pulp writer! And I'm not going away. I've published a Secret Agent X tale in Volume 2 of that series along with the Jim tale you just read. And Mars McCoy is on the horizon. Who is Mars McCoy? Go to whiterocketbooks.com to find out. And that's just the beginning! I've found a home here -- a place where I can write and publish pulp fiction for the growing audience out there, people like you, dear reader. I only hope that this tale and the others entertain the reader gracious enough to pick them up. If you've made it this far, all I can say is thanks for being there and I hope you enjoyed the story. See you next time.

As for the Crimson Scorpion, have we seen the last of him? That's up to you. Let your voice be heard if you want to see more. Just sneak a peek over your shoulder from time to time. To be safe.

ANDREW SALMON Ellis Award nominee Andrew Salmon lives and writes in Vancouver, Canada. His short work has appeared in numerous magazines, including Parsec, Storyteller, TBT, Thirteen Stories and online at thedeepening.com and blazingadventures.com. He also writes reviews for The Comicshopper. And he is currently writing a superhero serial novel for A Thousand Faces magazine.

His first book, *The Forty Club*, was a critical and commercial success and he followed it with *The Dark Land*, which Pulp Fiction Reviews called *"a straight out science-fiction thriller that fires on all cylinders."* Airship 27/Cornerstone Books have just released his new novel, *The Light Of Men* -- a time travel adventure set in a Nazi concentration camp. A sequel to *The Dark Land* is currently in the works as is his first children's book, *Wandering Webber* with illustrator Maki Naro.

Along with *"Death Walks Behind You"* his Secret Agent X story, *"The Icarus Terror"*, appeared in Volume 2 of Airship 27's series. He will also have a story in the upcoming *Mars McCoy* anthology from Airship27/White Rocket Books. For more information on Andrew Salmon and his work, check out http://stores.lulu.com/andrewsalmon.

JIM ANTHONY

in

Curse of the Red Jaguar

by B. C. Bell

Chapter I
Rise of the Jaguar

Eduardo Valenzuela had the blood of kings in his veins and never even knew it. For seven generations his family had lived and worked on the Yucatan Peninsula, some fishing, some farming, some hunting. Eduardo himself had been a farmer when the white men came down from the North. Some generations back, explorers had discovered an ancient civilization in the rain forest. Never mind that Eduardo's family had known it was there all along.

So now, years later, Eduardo had gone to work for the archeologists, doing the real work. Everyday he would dig, all day long, beneath the unforgiving Central American sun, tunneling deep into the earth while the white men would sit and sometimes brush at one stone for hours. Then they would suddenly become enthralled as a picture of a snake or a bird was revealed. Eduardo didn't mind; the deeper he dug, the cooler the earth was. And usually when one of his employers discovered a new carving, Eduardo would get to take a break, and he would tell them everything he knew about the stories carved in the rock—stories about the plumed-snake, and the lizard-god, the javelina and the jaguar. There were lots of stories about the jaguar.

The panther of the rain forest was the deadliest hunter in all of the Yucatan, sometimes sitting camouflaged in the low limbs of the trees for hours, before pouncing on its unsuspecting victim on the trail below. Men from the North always died this way, until they learned to bring dogs with them. A man without a dog, the jaguar didn't even have to pounce on him. The jaguar, she merely waited, and as the man rode under, she would swat him with her claws. The man's horse would run, and the man was usually already dead. If not, well, at least the most terrifying part of his life would be brief.

Eduardo's family had hunted down the big cats for as long as they had been there, using only a spear and the dogs. But Eduardo was no fool. Digging holes for the archeologists was much safer, and it paid more than farming. Much more.

However, in many cases it was easier for him to plant the food than it was to go to town and buy it. So Eduardo had never stopped farming. His wife and children had done a good deal of the work while he had been digging, but as always, harvest time had come and he had been forced to take a few days off to work the farm. Now he was headed back to the site of the dig so he could work some more. He could not bring his dogs to the site, because they would rile the hounds of the archeologists. So he walked through the jungle-like flora of the rainforest, and as he made his way down to the old Mayan plaza, he read the stories that the trail told him with its every bent leaf and broken branch. Every piece of bark and every twig was an encyclopedia of information to Eduardo.

Eduardo kept his ears open as he headed down the trail, listening for the things his eyes could not see. The call of the birds, the cry of a monkey, the slap of the iguana's feet upon the ground, all these things could warn one of the coming of a forest predator. Everything seemed safe as he headed up the hill to the site of the dig. The sound of men screaming and gunfire echoed through the valley. And then, everything was still. The entire rain-forest seemed silent except for the slapping sound of the big lizards running away, unseen, through the foliage.

Eduardo crawled behind some brush at the edge of the clearing near the ancient pyramid that the northerners called the Castillo. None of the dogs that were normally kept tied up at the edge of the plaza were visible. Nor were they barking. As silently as possible, Eduardo began to circle the great temple, making sure to keep to the edge of the forest so that he wouldn't be seen. A pack of dogs lay slaughtered off to the west, still leashed to the corner of the structure, teeth exposed, eyes staring at the sun, the blood drying beneath them. Everything lay hushed, dead silent. The archeologists were nowhere to be seen. Slowly, Eduardo edged as far as he could to the north. When the lack of foliage forced him to stop, he could feel the shadow of death hanging over the Castillo.

Eduardo had felt death here many times before and had always written it off as mere superstition. Maybe it was some scrap of genetic memory. Maybe it was a trace of his unknown ancestors that had witnessed death in this place long before. Or maybe it was simply the fact that he was one with this land. But something, something sent a chill down Eduardo's spine, and told him to stay hidden.

A man emerged from the top of the ancient pyramid. He stood atop the altar, gazing around the plaza as if it were his. Shirtless, he wore tan jodhpurs and brown boots. There was blood on his bare, white chest. He was one of the men from the North, but he wore a wide, golden belt that resembled armor. And instead of the pith helmets and caps that seemed uniform among these explorers, he wore a native headdress. It was tall and red, decorated with rows of feathers, and under its many adornments stood the crown of a king.

Eduardo shivered as the stranger turned slowly toward him. The poor dirt farmer and laborer, a man whose relatives had once ruled this place, sank as far back in the bush as he could without rustling the leaves. He didn't know why, for surely he could not be seen. And yet the man seemed to looking directly at him.

The strange foreigner slowly turned to face directly north. He raised both arms in the air as if in victory, like he was looking down at the masses that once filled this plaza. And as he did so, a gigantic black panther hopped out of the doorway at the top of the altar behind him, and gracefully sauntered up to the man's side. At the edge of the shadowy entrance, another panther came into to view. It sat down, chewing on a large piece of meat. The strange man from the North finally kneeled on his haunches and put one arm around the neck of the jaguar as if it were his pet. Or as if he were merely another jaguar. Then he stood again, turning back and forth and raising his arms to the imaginary crowd. Eduardo noticed something in one of his hands he hadn't seen before. The man in the red crown held a human head up, his hands clenched around the hair.

He held it up for the panther to smell. The black devil licked at it, trying to reach the blood of the severed neck. Then the stranger held the head in both hands, as if looking into the corpses eyes. And dropkicked it.

The head plopped off the steps almost halfway down, and from there popped and wobbled as it bounced down the remainder of the seventy-eight foot pyramid. The panther bounded back and forth, chasing the flopping head from one direction to the next. There were ninety-one steps on each side of the temple. The jaguar had the head in its jaws before it hit the ninetieth.

An hour later Eduardo ran into the house out of breath and excited. He grabbed his wife Dorina, and pulled her away from the pots on the wood burning stove. He held both her shoulders so she couldn't turn away and looked her directly in the eyes before he told her what they had to do.

"Dorina, hurry, you must gather all the children. Gather blankets, and pack. We have to go to town. We cannot stay."

"But Eduardo, what is it?"

"La Jaguar Roja!"

Chapter II
Enter the Manhunter

She was tall, lithe, and blonde. And dressed in cherry red from head to toe, she had the attention of every man in the lounge at the world famous Waldorf-Anthony Hotel.

Tom Gentry, the freckle-faced aviator, driver and trained agent, hadn't come downstairs to the lounge to look for a date, but he couldn't take his eyes off the blonde. The woman wasn't just stunning, she was a knockout.

His eyes focused on her ankle-strapped high heels and followed a firm, muscular calf-line all the way up her slit skirt and over her hips—barely making it around the curves of her bosom—to almost drown in the blue of her eyes. If she hadn't been wearing a stand-out, long brimmed hat, he probably wouldn't have made it up that far. Regardless, he'd forgotten what he came downstairs for.

"Excuse me, sir. May I help you," the woman at the bar asked him.

Gentry blushed when he realized he must have been staring. Then he realized he still was, all the while standing there with his mouth open. "Oh, uh, sorry. No, I thought I recognized you for a second there, but, uh, well, then I realized you were too good looking... I mean, I realized you, well, you were better looking than—what I meant to say was—" Gentry, who had made passes at women on at least six different continents, had been caught off guard.

The blonde stunner giggled.

"Oh heck, what I meant to say was you're really pretty." Gentry offered, shuffling his feet and staring down at them in a sarcastic effort to make fun of his flabbergasted lack of debonair. It was an approach that had worked for him in the past.

She giggled some more. Gentry looked up at her, surprised, and grinned. He could really go for this gal. "Hiya, I'm Tom Gentry, and you are...?"

"Eleanor. Eleanor Fontaine," she said, offering her hand, "Pleased to meet you."

"Oh, I'm pleased to meet you, Eleanor Fontaine," Gentry said her name as if he were reading it off a marquee, took her hand and bowed. "Um, excuse me, miss. I'm not trying to put the moves on you or anything, but I came down to the lounge 'cause I was getting bored upstairs—"

"As was I, Mr. Gentry." Tom's imagination began to run away with him, all the way upstairs.

"Well, so I came down here because I needed a change of scenery, but I still want to try to catch my boss before he gets upstairs and gets all wrapped up in his science experiments."

"Really. Science experiments? In a hotel?"

"You betcha, Miss Fontaine. He's really a brilliant guy, but once he starts playing around with those test tubes and wires, well, sometimes he'll be up days before I can get his attention around to business. So, anyway, I was kind of wondering—and this isn't a line or anything—but I was wondering if you might come up to the penthouse with me. We could listen to the radio, or play some cards or—"

The blonde's eyes opened wide. "The penthouse! Waitaminnit, you're boss isn't Jim Anthony is he?"

This was the part Tom Gentry hated. He had been doing his best not to mention Jim's name, but unfortunately, anybody that could read a newspaper knew Jim Anthony was headquartered out of the forty-fourth floor penthouse of the hotel bearing his last name. Tom did all right with the girls by himself, but as soon as a certain type—like this blonde, for instance—knew he worked for Jim Anthony, suddenly he was minor league. Dames like this always went all goo-goo eyed when they had a chance to meet a celebrity like Jim Anthony.

Jim was an investigator and manhunter of international prominence. The swarthy half-Comanche, half-Irish detective was blessed not only with amazing physical ability, but with an insatiable curiosity—a curiosity that had made him an expert in half a hundred sciences. His father, adventurer Sean Boru Anthony, had seen himself in these traits and had hired thousands of tutors from all over the world to satiate Jim's quest for knowledge while growing up. Jim Anthony was a man of science, a solver of mysteries, a hunter of men. And while he never chased the spotlight, his exploits invited it. It didn't it hurt that his father had also left him a fortune.

"Why, I would just love to join you, Mr. Gentry." Her eyes almost melted Tom, who hadn't even had a chance to answer her question, but was about to walk out of the lounge with one of the most beautiful women in Manhattan. Yeah, it wasn't easy working for a guy like Jim Anthony—but there were definitely worse jobs in the world, too.

Tom offered the lady his arm, just as a lanky, young man in a pork pie hat jumped up from one of the seats behind him, ran across the lobby and grabbed him by the shoulder.

"Hey, red! Where ya think you're going with my girl?"

This was the other thing that usually went with girls of a certain type like this blonde, Tom thought, turning to face the man. "Just taking a little stroll, buddy. And as far as her being 'your girl,' you might want to ask her. I'm pretty sure slavery is illegal."

"Oh, Billy! Not now!" The blonde stunner behind Gentry's back said, almost whining.

Yup, she was that type. Jealous boyfriend.

The young man's chin dug into his throat and his eyes widened as if offended. He inhaled sharply; a sure telegraph to a fighter like Tom Gentry, telling him that the kid was about to do something stupid. 'Billy' took a swing at Tom.

Tom looked as if he were bowing to the lad as he politely ducked, wrapping his arms about the kid's waist like he was going to tackle him. Gentry then raised the youth up on his shoulder, and gently flipped him over his back, almost letting him slide to the floor. Tom Gentry was not going to start any trouble in the Waldorf-Anthony; it was just too nice a place.

Before Gentry could even turn around to face his opponent, something else got his attention—along with everybody else in the lounge.

A man had walked in.

Dressed in baggy slacks and a T-shirt, most men would command no more attention than your average construction worker on his way to work. But this man, there was something about his presence that seemed to fill the room. There was nothing overtly unusual about his outward appearance, other than the knapsack on his back, and the fact that he wore huaraches instead of shoes. And yet, he seemed to exude a certain strength, an aura of energy, that made others aware of Jim Anthony.

Jim stopped in the lounge's entryway, pushing back his well-trimmed, jet black hair with one hand to neaten it. It flopped back on his head in its usual happenstance fashion. One couldn't help but notice the light of intelligence burning in his onyx-colored eyes as he glanced over his shoulder at the backpack, as if that was what was calling attention to him. Women visibly swooned, even the knockout blonde made a squeaking sound. The room was quiet for a second before everyone went back to pretending that nothing could impress a New Yorker.

Jim Anthony's muscular, yet lean, athletic body, resembled the copper figure sitting atop a championship trophy. He was not handsome in the traditional sense. His eyes, for example, seemed a little too deep set behind high cheekbones he had inherited from his mother, Fawn Johntom, a Comanche princess. His hawk-like nose seemed to cut the air along with a rugged jaw line and strong chin. Jim smiled and strolled across the floor toward Tom Gentry.

Billy, the jilted lover, stopped in his tracks behind Tom when he recognized Jim Anthony. He stood there looking angry for a second before he looked up at his raised fist like it belonged to somebody else, and then, slowly, cupped one hand in the other.

"You alright, kid?" Jim said. He was talking to Tom but the young man in the background, Billy, suddenly glanced to both sides, looking self conscious. He bent down and picked up his pork pie hat, before he inched back toward the blonde.

"I spent all morning trying to find you and you were gone. You musta got up and left at O-dark-thirty," Tom said, seeming to forget all about Billy.

"I'd been up all night when I remembered the project I'd been working on with the ICPC," Jim said, not bothering to translate the name of the now defunct International Police Department. "I'd given up on it since the Nazi's annexed Austria, but I figured why not finish and give the info to the F.B I. Would you believe I hadn't taken a soil sample from the Bronx yet?"

Foot-long, glass tubes, corked and full of dirt, were holstered in belts on the sides of Jim's backpack. Jim reached behind his head and unholstered one of the tubes like he was pulling an arrow out of its quiver. His eyes transformed into polished basalt, gleaming with enthusiasm as he showed the tube of dirt to Tom.

"You gotta get out more, Pappy." Tom said. "Honest, I never seen anybody get so excited over a tube full of dirt." The two men walked back toward the bar, and Tom waved the bartender over. "Give me another, Don. And a…"

"Orange juice," Jim said.

"And an orange juice for the dirt collector! Toot sweet, my man!"

The bartender laughed, he'd already set up a blender full of fresh squeezed for Jim. The Waldorf-Anthony had a reputation for service second to none.

"It might be just a tube full of dirt to you, Tom. But imagine what we could do with soil samples from all over the world."

"Build a sand castle?" Tom shoved a coaster over to Jim before the bartender had a chance to.

"No. Don't you get it? Or do you just not care?"

"Actually, I do care, Jim. I really do. But I'm also trying to get that blonde over there's number, without breaking pork pie's heart."

"Stunning isn't she?" Jim sipped at his orange juice

"I didn't think you'd notice. Figured she'd have to roll in the dirt and jump in a test tube to get your attention."

"I didn't want to break pork pie's heart, either," Jim said, smiling. He took off his pack and set it down on the floor beside him.

"Besides," Tom said, "you didn't ask me why I was looking for you all morning."

Jim pulled a newspaper out of his pack and tossed it on the bar. It was folded open to reveal the headline: Bank Baron Missing, Police Suspect Foul Play. Large print beneath the headline read: Millionaire Benson Prescott's Whereabouts Unknown.

"You read my mind, Pappy." Tom was still watching the blonde out of the corner of his eye. "Don't you know this Prescott guy?"

"I've met him. He's a member of the Explorer's Club that meets here in the hotel, although he hasn't been around too much since his wife died. A self made man— oil business—became a bank owner, investments in everything from radio to steel. Also known to be a ruthless businessman, made a lot of enemies. "

"I knew it. You're practically working on this one already. Ya wanna check it out?"

In Penthouse A, on the forty-fourth floor of the Waldorf-Anthony, a strange ceremony was beginning. A frighteningly thin old man, dressed only in buckskins, placed nine, burning, wooden sticks in the grate of the fireplace. His flesh looked like the skin of a drum wrapped around a skeleton, and yet somehow managed to hold thousands of wrinkles at the same time. It would have been hard to tell where the buckskin ended and the old man began if his ribcage hadn't stuck out like the staves of a barrel. His gnarled, ancient hands rearranged the narrow sticks of burning wood, and he smiled revealing black, toothless gums. This was Mephito, Comanche shaman, father of Fawn Johntom and Grandfather of Jim Anthony. Only God knew how old he was.

The old man squatted over the small fire, his beady little eyes half open, and began to chant in sounds that were more rhythm than song. Reaching into the medicine bag at his hip, he began to feed herbs, tobacco and tiny monstrosities into the fire.

A small, stooped figure, dressed in tuxedo and tails ran into the room with a silver serving tray in his hand. For a second it looked like he was going to hit the old man over the head with it. Dawkins, Jim's butler, had been fighting a minor war of cultures with Mephito for years now. Originally, he had thought the old mummy to be crazy. Since then, he had found a great, but grudging, respect for the old man's knowledge, as it was often as nearly as dependable as Jim's scientific fact. Both men's experiments tended to frustrate and confound the butler's cockney sensibilities.

"Mephito! H'oh no! I just finished h'airing out the stink from the last fire you started. H'i know Mister Anthony h'is used to it, but h'i am certainly not, and h'if guests should h'arrive— Oh my, what's that?"

"Dried frog," Mephito said. One could almost detect the beginnings of a smile when Dawkins made a face.

"Good God, h'it's going to smell like somebody set h'a bait shop on fire h'in here."

Mephito held an adder's tongue up in front of Dawkin's face and threw it on the fire. A bell chimed as Jim Anthony and Tom Gentry entered. Without the knockout blonde.

"I'm tellin' ya, pappy. All you had to do is ask and Miss Fontaine would be up here fanning you and feeding you grapes like—"

"We've got other business to attend to right now, Tom, besides, if you insist I'll be

"…h'it's going to smell like somebody set h'a bait shop on fire…"

glad to take her phone number from you."

"H'excuse me, sir," Dawkins said. "H'i don't mean to interrupt your discussion h'on the semantics h'of 'uman sociology and h'agriculture, but might you require some midday repast before your grandfather's nasal h'insensitivity kills your appetite?"

"Bring some sandwiches and tea for me, Dawkins," Jim said, reaching for the phone. "Give Tom and Mephito whatever they want."

"I'll have a brandy," Tom said. "Stinkin' the joint up with the mojo again, eh Mephito?"

The old man ignored Gentry's comment and maintained his stoic composure. "You got any worms, Dawkins?"

"Not h'even if you were starving," the butler replied, knowing full well that the shaman wanted them for the fire.

"Hello, operator," Jim said, into the phone. "Give me the Daily Star, city desk." The Star was not only one of New York's most competitive daily papers, but Jim Anthony was also its chief shareholder. "Hello, McMahon? This is Anthony, I need everything you've got on Benson Prescott, including the reporter's notes on his missing person case, if you can get them. Send it over by courier if you have to ASAP."

Gentry and Mephito concentrated on the food and drink Dawkins had brought in, while Anthony quickly made a call to Police Commissioner Carrothers.

"Commissioner, Jim Anthony. I was wondering if I might look into the Benson Prescott case. Have you searched his house yet?" Commissioner Carrothers, who had actually asked for Anthony's advice on previous cases, welcomed Jim to the investigation and said he'd have an officer at Prescott's house to meet them in an hour. Gentry had to remind Jim to eat before they went to work.

On the way out Mephito stopped them.

"Jim, firesticks say Iktome, the spider, has been at work. All is not what it seems. Remember, Iktome is a dangerous trickster. Lightning will strike before you hear the thunder."

"We'll wear our galoshes," Tom Gentry joked, but they all knew Mephito's warning was dead serious.

Chapter III
Judge, Jury and Executioner

Benson Prescott's home was both a declaration of, and a monument to wealth. An ostentatious, gothic mansion, it was surrounded by Roman pillars, easily a foot wide in diameter, that served to make the front of the estate look like the entrance to a small coliseum. The front porch was larger than most people's homes. Jim took in the sheer size of the place, and wondered if Prescott ever found time to actually enjoy any of it.

After driving through the front gate, Tom parked a seemingly nondescript sedan directly behind a police car in the circular driveway. Jim stepped out and opened the trunk, removing a thick leather case, similar to one a salesman might carry samples in. He'd brought his own version of a portable crime lab with him just in case. The two of them climbed a series of wide, stone steps to the front door of the monolithic monstrosity, where a stout man in a wrinkled suit, chewing a cigar waited for them. They were fifteen minutes early, but Lieutenant Trotter looked like he'd been waiting all day.

"Y'know Anthony, if I was you, I'd be out living it up like this guy instead of driving the local police crazy with your little crimebusting hobby," Trotter said. Trotter and Anthony had locked horns with each another on more than one occasion in the past. The Lieutenant seemed to resent the fact that Jim had solved most of those cases—even though Trotter usually got most of the credit.

"Lieutenant Trotter, I'm surprised to see you here," Jim said. "This isn't a homicide."

"Yet," Trotter said, around the cigar butt. "My theory—the guy just got fed up and flew off to Hawaii or something, and they'll find him in about a week, sitting on the beach in his water wings. Meanwhile, I get pulled off real cases so I can look for Mister Millionaire and baby-sit you amateurs."

"Just trying to earn my keep, Trotter," Anthony said. "You know, of course, the Latin root for the word amateur means enthusiastic. It really doesn't refer to the professionalism of the practitioner. It just means I don't get paid."

"Yeah, sure. 'Course I know that. Just sometimes I forget all that Latin I learned in medical school—before I decided to walk a beat. C'mon." Trotter ripped the crime scene tape down and unlocked the door.

Jim Anthony and Tom Gentry followed him into the foyer. The room was enormous. Dark oak, French doors stood on both sides of the entry hall, next to wide matching staircases that met on a balcony in the center of the room, twenty feet above the black and white mosaic tile where they stood. Tom Gentry opened one of the French doors exposing a gauche, white living room laden with more dark oak furniture and a carpet so deep you could have lost your feet in it.

"Wow, look at the size of this place," Gentry said. "You could hold a convention in here."

"Take a convention just to clean the place," Trotter said.

"Police already go over everything here?" Jim said, getting to business.

"With a fine tooth." Trotter blew a cloud of blue-gray smoke up the stairs. "Three sets of prints. Two from the help. We're assuming the other set is Prescott's; he's got no prints on record, and they're all over the office."

"Born outside New York, I take it. No birth certificate?" Jim said, looking up the staircase.

"Nope. We sent a request to state archives out on the teletype," Trotter said. "But a lot of the other forty-eight didn't start issuing birth ID 'til the teens. And if he was born abroad…"

Something tensed inside of Jim. He noticeably stiffened as if every nerve and muscle in his amazing body had been alerted. Jim's sixth sense, an almost gut feeling that he had never been able to adequately describe, was one of the things that made him such a remarkable detective. An odd sensation that warned Jim of danger, it also quite often called his attention to tiny details on a case—details that might seem of no importance at the time, but would later point him in the right direction. Jim had often wondered if perhaps this strange extrasensory ability wasn't some sort of warning system passed down from his Comanche ancestors. An ancient genetic holdover from the days of hunters and hunted when a predator could become prey just by being in the wrong place at the wrong time.

The problem was Jim didn't know what it meant. He knew something had occurred, or was about to occur, but he didn't know what. He scanned the room but there were no signs of danger. Something was pulling him upstairs.

"Is there an office up there?" Jim angled his head toward the steps.

"Hey, for an amateur detective you're pretty good." Trotter pulled the cigar stub out of his mouth and gestured to the right with it. "End of the hall, don't track on the carpet."

By the time Trotter and Gentry made it upstairs, Jim had already been standing in the office doorway for several moments. He held his arms out from his sides preventing anybody from entering the room as he made a mental note of everything in it. The walls were paneled with even more of the same dark oak and several bookshelves, filled mostly with texts on finance and exploration, sat between the two windows. A large set of wooden file cabinets stood behind a large oak desk, and a bar with a seltzer bottle and glasses on it sat on the opposite side of the room. A couch, two leather chairs and a coffee table sat in the center. You could see where the police had dusted for prints.

Trotter exhaled impatiently. "May I?" he said, trying to push Jim's hand out of the way.

Jim held him back another second then lowered his arm. Trotter went right in and sat on the front of the big oak desk before saying, "It's an office." Tom headed for the bar.

Jim stood in the center of the room and turned slowly as if looking for ghosts. He stared down at the coffee table briefly before he opened his briefcase and pulled out a box of rubber gloves. He removed a pair and threw the box over to Tom, who caught it on the fly before it had a chance to land on the bar.

Tom snapped the gloves on and said, "What'll ya have, Pappy?" pulling a bottle of whiskey out of the rack and starting to pour himself a glass.

"Nothing yet," Jim Anthony said. "It might be drugged." Tom's eyes widened, he looked at the bottle, then at the glass and back again. He let out a heavy sigh and put the whiskey back in the rack.

Trotter smiled, and said: "Lab boys took samples, they're going over it." He stuck his cigar in the ashtray and pulled two more out of his coat, holding one up in the air, offering it to Gentry. Tom walked over to the desk and took the cigar, waved it under his nose and gave Trotter a thumbs up sign.

Jim continued to turn, slowly looking over the room, memorizing it. Briefly, he closed his eyes, filing away his mental blueprint of the office. "And you found nothing," he said.

"Like I said, squat." Trotter handed a box of matches to Gentry, whose glance followed Jim Anthony's around the room.

No slouch as a detective himself, Tom Gentry still preferred action to deduction. At times like this he enjoyed standing back and watching Jim work his magic. Anthony continued to turn slowly and then stopped facing the bar. He walked over behind it and knelt down.

"Whoa there, Jimmy boy. I thought you said the liquor might be poisoned?" Tom said, walking over. Trotter ambled up from behind, blowing a smoke ring in the air and watching it disintegrate, before finally furrowing his brow in curiosity as he looked down at Anthony on the floor. Jim was facing the wall, staring at the polished oak baseboard. He ran his hand across the top of it as if looking for dust.

"I told ya, Anthony, we went over this room with a fine tooth comb," the lieutenant said.

Jim turned his head to the side, still facing the wall. He stood up, walked over to the corner and knelt again, brushing the top of the baseboard with his fingers.

"I'll be glad to let ya look at the files, even," Trotter went on. "Send over all the lab resul—"

Jim Anthony had pressed part of the baseboard down into a groove in the floor, before it bounced back into place as if levered with a spring. A section of paneling slid to the side revealing a hidden wall safe.

The lieutenant's jaw hung open in amazement for only a moment, before he caught himself and chomped down on the cigar in an angry grimace. He caught himself again and almost smiled, laughing at himself, as he pushed his hat back on his head. "Well I'll be damned."

Tom Gentry clapped his hands together. "Now were getting somewhere."

"Lemme get a hold of headquarters on the phone," Trotter said. "We'll have a locksmith out here to open the thing within the hour. If not we'll call the manufacturer and—" The lieutenant realized both men were staring at him shaking their heads. "You're gonna crack the safe, aren't ya?"

Tom Gentry's eyebrows went up before he asked: "Can you?"

"As long as the lieutenant's here I'm sure it's perfectly legal," Jim said, smiling at Trotter in a sarcastic fashion. Trotter chewed more cigar than he smoked, making grumbling noises underneath his breath.

"I meant 'can you' in a will-you-be-able-to or is-it-possible kind of way," Tom said.

"Good luck, that's a state of the art Moesler you're looking at there. It may look small, but the doors prob'ly thicker than the wall," Trotter said. "And you're not gonna blow the thing on my watch. City of New York's got enough damage on the books without you millionaire playboy types running to the fireworks stand."

Instead of answering, that curious light gleamed in Jim Anthony's eyes again. He stepped briskly back over to the portable crime lab and, after opening the bottom, revealed a small black box about the size of a dry cell battery, with what looked like a stethoscope running through it. Placing the earpieces around his neck, he held the box up, letting the metal disc dangle in the air from its rubber tubing.

"Gentleman, I give you the Anthony Sound Amplifier," Jim said, placing the earpieces around his neck. "I haven't had time to modify the design so it still looks like a cigar box with a stethoscope glued to it but, given that I've modified it with my own special electron tube, it should be able to magnify any sound by at least a hundred times. The applications are endless, for instance when attached to a directional microphone an ordinary man could listen in on a conversation a block away. Or in this case, to the muted tumblers of a combination lock."

Tom Gentry rolled his eyes the moment Jim uttered the words "electron tube." Ever since Anthony had seen the demonstration of a photoelectric eye, he had spent half his time modifying the "little glass wonders," and installed them all over the penthouse. Poor Dawkins had been forced to relearn how to use every appliance in the kitchen, and you couldn't step into a room in the penthouse without the lights coming on automatically. Between Mephito's medicine man routine and Jim's gadgets, it was almost spooky.

Trotter made a harrumphing sound and said, "I'm gonna go ahead and contact headquarters, try to get the lab boys back out here. Maybe even get the Moesler people on it, just in case. You boys have fun. I'll be right back."

Jim Anthony was already standing in front of the safe, making a shushing motion, holding his fingers to his lips. Apparently he didn't want any background noise filtering through. Unaided Jim's hearing was already fantastically acute, in the past he had solved cases by merely hearing suspects whisper in another room. Amplified, a sudden noise might even harm the hearing of the super-detective.

After turning the volume dial to zero, Jim flipped an electric switch on top of the Anthony Sound Amplifier, and a tiny red light came on. He placed the earpieces in his ears and gradually turned the dial just above the "two" marker. With the metal disc of the amplifier pointed into the air he could hear Lieutenant Trotter's footsteps on the other side of the house.

"Do me a favor Tom, and don't move," Jim said. "I can hear the inside of your pockets rustle against the fabric of your pants with this thing on." Tom looked down at his pants like they had done something wrong.

Jim turned the volume back down to zero, placed the disc of the stethoscope just below the safe's dial, and then turned the volume up again. Every click was defined. When the tumblers dropped it sounded like somebody had opened a floodgate. Within two minutes Jim Anthony was taking off the amplifier. He reached for the lock handle and, with a firm click that would have deafened him only a second ago, pulled the safe door open.

Tom hurried to look over Jim's shoulder, inside the safe. It was empty except for a note scrawled on a piece of typing paper. Jim Anthony picked the scrap of paper up gently, by the edges, as if it were a piece of ancient papyrus he was afraid would crumble at his touch. "Clear the desktop off, would you?"

Tom moved the ashtray, and wiped the desk blotter off with the edge of his hand. Jim sidled over, smoothly laying the piece of paper down, pressing the top and bottom lightly to keep it from folding closed. The two of them stared down at the note for several minutes. Written in a sepia-red that resembled dried blood, each sentence was written in a different font—some in cursive lettering, some in block, the signature a barely legible scrawl. It read:

From Above,
Benson Prescott is mine. I am the judge, jury, and executioner if I so choose. The weigher of souls. The thief of fire. Let those who threaten my empire fear—
—The Red Jaguar

One of Jim's eyebrows came down, his eye almost squinting as if trying to see something before he said, "Get me a loupe out of the briefcase."

Tom dug around in the portable crime lab looking for the jeweler's magnifier. Jim sat down at the desk and continued to stare at the note with one hand on his chin, his index finger thoughtlessly rubbing just below his mouth. His left eye, like burning onyx, was still slit as if already holding the loupe

"Seems to be written on ordinary rice paper. My guess is it's a printer's ink. If the writer used real blood, he would have had to thin it to write legibly and it would have faded more. Not that it's all that legible, anyway. Look at the extremes. It's like four different people wrote this. Half of it is perfect penmanship, in two different styles. The other half—I'm surprised it's not scrawled in crayon."

As Tom handed the loupe to Jim, Lieutenant Trotter swung open the office door. Standing halfway in the entrance with his hand still on the knob, he said, "We got trouble, boys! Stephen Hanlon's life has been threatened—this time for ransom. Some guy, calls himself—"

"The Red Jaguar," Jim Anthony said.

Chapter IV
Death Writes in Red

Tom Gentry had no problem speeding to the luxury apartment of Mr. Stephen Hanlon. He knew exactly where it was because Hanlon lived in the penthouse of a luxury high rise, directly across the street from the Waldorf-Anthony. On the drive over, Jim had thumbed through his mental rolodex and given Tom Gentry a detailed rundown on Stephen Hanlon's background. Jim knew Hanlon as a member of the Explorer's Club and, since the steel magnate regularly appeared on both the sports and business pages, Tom already knew most of it.

A University of Illinois Alumni football player, Stephen Hanlon had been offered a career in the pros much like Red Grange. Fortunately for him, after a knee injury left him unable to play, Hanlon had taken a job at his father's steel mill—a much more financially rewarding venture in the long run, especially since he was now president of the United American Steel Company. He was also a world record holding safari hunter and member of the New York chapter of the Explorer's Club, just like Benson Prescott had been. Unlike Prescott, he was a family man with a wife and four children.

Tom Gentry's expert driving had gotten them to Manhattan within a half-hour. It had taken Trotter another half hour to catch up in the evening traffic. Mr. Hanlon had forced both Jim and Tom to stay out in the hall until Trotter had arrived, even though the police officer already stationed at the door had assured him it was the real Jim Anthony. It was dusk when the three men finally entered the millionaire explorer's Fifth Avenue apartment.

Stephen Hanlon sat in an overstuffed blue chair, at a glass table in the center of the room, a cigarette in one hand, and a Luger tucked between his leg and the armrest. Now in his thirties, his hair was beginning to thin. He was pale, turgid, and constantly wiping a reappearing sheen of sweat off his brow with a monogrammed handkerchief, as he drank from a glass of pale brown liquor to soothe his nerves. For someone who had gained fame confronting risk in both business and pleasure, he seemed very unnerved—probably because both were now in jeopardy.

Hanlon remained seated; his hand ready to reach for the gun as Lieutenant Trotter and Tom Gentry began to pace back and forth, both asking questions at the same time. Jim Anthony pulled a straight back chair away from the wall and sat down with his legs straddled around the back of it, directly across from Hanlon. His voice, while not as loud as Tom's or Trotter's, seemed to demand immediate attention. Hanlon wiped his forehead, after sipping from his drink and setting it down again.

"Do you know, or have you heard anything about this Red Jaguar before?" Jim asked. "Do you know anybody with a similar name, or have you ever heard anyone reference a 'Red Jaguar' before?"

"No. Never, Jim. I've been scouring my thoughts since I called the police. I can't even come up with anything referencing a red bird—except maybe the St. Louis Cardinals, and I've never even been to one of their games. Still, it does sound like a sports thing to me. Maybe a nickname, y'know?"

"You have any old football rivalries? Somebody that may want to hurt you?"

"That was years ago, Jim. And as far as anybody holding a grudge—I'm the one that got sidelined. Far as I know I never did any long term damage to anyone."

"Have you got any business enemies you know of?" Jim said.

"Possibly, some I don't know about. I mean, that's business. I never expected anybody to threaten my life," Hanlon said, handing the ransom note to Jim across the table. Another red ink blurb in a wide range of handwriting. This one read:

Hanlon—

Place 1 million $—in unmarked bills—in a black satchel and bring it to Grand Central Station. Alone. No cops. Main Concourse. Drop it in the wastebasket beneath Orion, the hunter. Tomorrow. 8:30 AM. Sharp. And I may let you live.

If not. Suffer the little children. And the wife.

—The Red Jaguar

"...have you heard anything about this Red Jaguar before?"

"If it were only me I wouldn't worry, but Lucille and the children…" Hanlon stared into his drink.

"Where are they now?" Trotter spit around his cigar.

"I decided she and the children would be safer staying at her parents' estate till this thing blew over. They're probably still on the plane to Chicago."

"Can I use your phone?" Trotter said. "I wanna notify the local police department to meet them at the airport. Put up a twenty-four hour guard."

"So they are in danger!" Hanlon glanced from one to the other of them.

"Not if we catch him first," Jim said. "Are you considering paying the ransom?"

"Of course. It's my family we're talking about here." Hanlon smashed his cigarette butt into the ashtray and immediately lit another, before reaching for his drink again.

"You might want to avoid drinking too heavily," Jim said. "I know you're tense, but we've got a lot of work to do before tomorrow."

At eight the next morning a nondescript sedan pulled just down the block from the front of Grand Central Station. Stephen Hanlon and Jim Anthony were seated in back. Tom Gentry sat in the front, wearing a chauffeur's hat as if he worked for Hanlon. In a matter of only a few hours Jim had choreographed a plan the night before, charting the floor plan of the concourse from memory. Working with Trotter they had arranged a timed patrol of the exits, with beat cops roving from exit to exit at each corner or directly across the street nearby. Undercover plainclothes detectives walked the floor pretending to be businessmen and tourists.

Jim had even donned a dark suit and hat, in hopes to blend in with the crowd a little better. He pointed at a penciled in map of the station as Hanlon reviewed the plan with his reading glasses on.

"All you have to do is walk into the station and sit down on the bench underneath the painted constellation of Orion on the ceiling," Jim said. "I should already be seated by the time Tom pulls in front of the station. If you should need a seat, I'll give you mine, throw away my newspaper and get a shoeshine. The shoe shine man is part of the Anthony organization, as will be numerous people walking all over the concourse."

The Anthony organization Jim referred to was of course the legendary Anthony legion. All over Manhattan, from lowly cleaning women up to captains of industry, one could find secret members of this uncommon regiment. Loyal adventurers who had at sometime in the past been pulled into Jim's battle against lawlessness and sworn their allegiance to the super-detective; an undercover army banded together to fight crime.

Jim Anthony exited the car fifteen minutes early, pulled his hat down low, covering his distinctive features and entered the main concourse of Grand Central Station. Five minutes before the drop was to be made Stephen Hanlon entered with a black satchel full of money. His eyes darted nervously among the crowd in hopes that his famed safari skill might somehow alert him to the presence of the Red Jaguar. Tom Gentry followed behind, having traded his chauffeur's garb for a racing form and cap that made him look like he was on his way to the track.

On any given day over a hundred-thousand people might walk through Grand Central Station. Even now the throng of the morning work crowd had already jammed the concourse, and all of the bench seats were taken. Jim stood up as Hanlon approached, folded his paper and pretended to brush off the top of his shoes, before his eyes met Hanlon's in silent reaffirmation. Anthony walked to the shoe shine stand quickly, somehow managing not to seem hurried. He sat down and nodded at the shoe shine man, who had kept lookout even as Jim's back had been turned. Jim pretended to look down at his shoes, the brim of his hat hiding his face.

At exactly 8:30 AM Stephen Hanlon rose from the bench and approached the nearby wastebasket. The hairs on the back of Jim Anthony's neck suddenly felt electrified as his famed sixth sense alerted him to unseen danger. Jim had known his genetic alarm system would call him to action before he even had a chance to know why. He had already planned his move ahead of time. He'd worn his belt.

While Jim Anthony carried a constant array of ever changing tools to aid him in his battle against evil, his belt was the one thing that never changed. To a casual observer the round, steel buckle might seem a bit odd, but other than that it looked like the ordinary leather strap any man uses to hold his pants up. It was in reality a long piece of tensile cord that retracted into a heavy, steel ball. Over the years Jim's belt had proven to be the most adaptable of tools. He had used it as an anchor and rope to climb walls; as a bolo for bringing down escaping felons; he had even fashioned nets out of cut sections of the cording. And at the end of the day, he could use it to tie up the bad guys.

Jim pressed the release on his belt buckle and stood up on top of the shoe shine stand. Now that his sixth sense had sounded the call to action he didn't have to worry about standing out, and from his perch atop the shoe shine stand he could keep an eye on most of the crowd. A tingle ran down his spine as a businessman wearing a long raincoat and carrying a cane strode briskly into his field of vision. It wasn't raining outside.

Jim stood behind the man watching as he approached Stephen Hanlon, who even now was carrying the satchel full of money across the floor. He peered over the businessman in the raincoat's shoulder just in time to see the gleaming blade of a stiletto pop out of the end of the cane. Anybody else would have been too far away to do anything. Jim Anthony was far from just anybody.

Holding onto the tensile cord strap, he hurled the steel ball at an outcropping wall hook used to hang seasonal decorations high on the concourse wall. With pinpoint accuracy the bolo-like steel ball spun itself over the iron hook to form a knot in the seemingly never ending cord, and Jim Anthony swung out over the crowd. He would only have one chance at this.

Flying through the air the daring detective kicked the raincoated killer off balance, even as he grabbed the deadly sword cane from his hand. Twisting in midair, Jim Anthony landed catlike in front of Hanlon holding the cane in both hands to ward of the murderer's attack. All Jim saw was the killer's raincoat as it finished its drop into a crumpled pile on the floor. His hat lay a few feet distant, being stepped over by the crowd.

"Stop that man! The one without a hat!" Jim bellowed over the crowd. Police jumped into the doorways. Secret members of the Anthony legion grabbed any stray passerby without a head covered.

Jim spun and grabbed Hanlon by the shoulders. "Are you all right?"

"Yes, I'm fine," Hanlon said. "You saw the killer?"

"Only his back. But I may be able to spot him out of the crowd."

Lieutenant Trotter charged in from the east entrance and had two men cordon off the area. Only to reveal Jim's undercover shoe shine man, who had been trying to follow the killer, knocked out and laying on the floor. Tom Gentry ran through the exit along with several more policemen, giving chase.

"You're sure you're OK?" Lieutenant Trotter asked Hanlon.

"Yes, yes, I'm fine. Please contact my family and make sure they're safe, though" Hanlon said.

"They're still under the guard of Chicago's finest," Trotter said, "but consider it done."

Surrounded by policemen, Trotter sat back down on the bench and lit a cigarette, running his hand through his hair as he sat back and watched the action. Tom Gentry came back on the concourse cursing under his breath.

"He got away clean, Jim. I'm sorry," the red-headed aviator said.

"It's not your fault, Tom. Sunny day like today, we can't exactly have the police going around arresting every man without a hat on." Jim turned and, walking toward the wall, began to retrieve his belt by scaling back up the cord like a mountaineer. Holding onto the decorative hook in the plaster, Jim unknotted his unique reeling belt buckle and tied the other end of the belt to the hook. Rappelling down the wall, he then cut the length of the belt with a pen knife and put it back on. He was walking to the information booth on the concourse, in order to leave an apology for the length of cord still hanging from the wall—when, once more, his sixth sense kicked in!

Every muscle in Jim Anthony's magnificent body went taut as he slowly turned to see Hanlon coughing and looking oddly at his cigarette. One of the policemen grabbed Hanlon by the collar and slapped him on the back. It didn't help. Hanlon loosened his tie and kept coughing. Jim rushed across the concourse as Hanlon dropped the cigarette and began clawing at his chest with both hands. His eyes opened wide as he began to collapse. Jim Anthony caught him and laid him on the ground. Hanlon made a rattling sound in the back of his throat. His wide eyes made one last conscious look at Jim, as if asking for help, before his body went limp.

Jim reached below Hanlon's ear with one hand and checked his pulse. "Ye gods! He's dead!"

Stunned policemen glanced to and fro at each other wondering what happened. What had gone wrong? Jim picked up the cigarette butt lying at Hanlon's feet. Sniffing it briefly, his finely tuned senses detected a faint almond odor.

"Cyanide. This man's been poisoned." Jim looked thunderstruck. This time it was him, not Tom Gentry, that was sorry. Jim Anthony had known Stephen Hanlon. He had dined with the man, even met his children. He had offered to protect his friend and he had failed. Jim's eyes turned to angry slits. He turned suddenly to Lieutenant Trotter. "I want a copy of everything you've got in evidence on this case. I want statements from Stephen's family as to who visited him in the last month. I want listings, Hanlon's and Prescott's business holdings and dealings—anything and everything! I'm bringing the Red Jaguar in!"

After several minutes of heated conversation, Trotter finally agreed to have the case files couriered over to the Waldorf-Anthony. Back at the hotel, Jim began to review his own notes and called the Daily Star's city desk to see if they had come up with anything on the case. As soon as he set the phone down it rang again.

"Mr. Anthony, this is Heath, the new house detective?" Jim Anthony assured the employee that he knew who he was. Heath continued, almost interrupting him. "I'm at the front desk. I know you left word that you weren't to be disturbed, but I thought you'd want to talk to this lady. She says she just got a death threat from the Red Jaguar."

"I want you to come up with her in the elevator, immediately," Jim said.

Tom Gentry was reclining on the couch at such an angle that if the coffee table had been two feet taller, he still could have put his feet up on it. He was going through a pack of cigarettes, sniffing them one by one to make sure he was safe. "You got the help sending women up for ya now, Pappy?"

"No, Tom." Jim said sounding bothered. "There's been another death threat."

Tom jumped upright and all his cigarettes fell on the floor. "Darn it!" It was hard to tell if he was complaining about the death threat or the tobacco. "Well, on the bright side, at least it's a girl. I mean, not that I'd want anything to happen to a girl either. It's just I'd much rather be in the company of—" Tom stopped talking, aware that Jim wasn't listening anyway. Tom had known Jim since childhood, and while usually Jim was the most chipper guy on earth, he was also prone to be obsessive. Whether it was about sports, science, business, or crime fighting, Jim Anthony was a man who gave everything he had. And right now he had a king-size case of the surly going on.

Ever since they had returned to the hotel, Jim had done nothing but pace back and forth, slamming doors as he walked from room to room, stopping only to write something else in his notes. He'd already called the police station twice, and the courier company once to ask why the case files weren't here yet. It was obvious to Tom he was both sad and angry about the death of Stephen Hanlon. Maybe if the girl couldn't pull him out of this mood, she'd have something else on the case that would.

The doorbell rang. Jim didn't even wait for Dawkins to come in. He opened it before the chime finished and motioned Detective Heath and the young lady in.

"Afternoon, Mr. Anthony"

"Detective Heath. Miss…?"

"Donne. Severana Donne, Mr Anthony." Her voice almost purred. Jim took her hand and bowed.

The second the auburn-haired heart-stopper had stepped one seductive leg into the room, Tom jumped up to meet her and spilled his cigarettes all over the floor again. She was petite, curvy, and athletic looking. She wore no makeup, but the dash of freckles that adorned her full cheeks and pert nose only served to accent luxurious, pink, pouty lips that complemented the rest of her porcelain skin. Dressed in a short, summer jumper with a sailor collar and red high heels she would have brought a rising temperature to any seaman lucky enough to call her shipmate—and this was all with a worried look on her face. If she had smiled the men lined up to meet her would have never let her make it upstairs.

"Sir, h'I do wish you would allow me time to greet h'and h'announce the guests." Dawkins had rushed up behind Jim. He looked once at Miss Donne and said, "H'especially one so lovely as this."

Miss Donne managed a smile and gave Dawkins a nod of greeting. Either the girl, or the fact that she had acknowledged him seemed to cheer the normally dour looking cockney. "Greetings to you also, Detective Heath. May I offer something to drink, sir?" Everyone agreed on coffee and Jim motioned for them to sit down.

Tom managed to get his cigarettes back in the pack and greeted Miss Donne by bowing and kissing her hand. Dawkins brought out a coffee tray with biscuits as everyone made themselves comfortable.

"So you're saying you received a death threat Miss Donne? May I ask where you were, what brought you here?"

"Why, I'm a guest here at the hotel. Room 503," she said. Her full bosom rose and fell as she spoke, as if she might be having trouble breathing. "I saw the extra in the paper this morning—about the tragedy at Grand Central—and since I knew you were on the case..."

"So you haven't contacted the police?" Jim said.

She licked her lips in anxiety and Tom almost fell out of his chair. "No, not yet—I wasn't sure. The note said not to."

"May I see it?" Jim said.

Severana pulled an envelope out of a matching navy handbag with an anchor embroidered on the side. Her name was scrawled in crimson on the paper like somebody had written it with a bloody icepick.

Jim took the note, holding the corners with the palms of his hand. Pulling a handkerchief out of his pocket, he used it to open the note on the coffee table. "Tom, could you go get a fingerprint kit?"

Tom didn't bother to mention they hadn't even gotten a partial sample yet, and grudgingly stepped into the lab. The note read.

To the Dawns—
Take the contract. And pay with your lives. I choose the victors. And victims.
—The Red Jaguar

"I don't even know what it means," Severana said.
"You wouldn't happen to be related to Mr. Robert Willis Donne, would you?" Jim

asked, still staring at the varied handwriting styles on the paper.

"Why yes, I am." Severana said.

"Whoa! You were related to old man Willis Donne, the shipping magnate?" Tom said, flopping back down on the couch as he threw the fingerprint kit on the coffee table. "I mean, Mr. Donne… Are related. The shipbuilder… who recently…"

"'Recently passed' is what I believe Mr. Gentry is trying to say," Jim finished. "Pardon my curiosity, but were you the only living heir?" Jim remembered the death of her mother from the newspaper but thought better than to bring that up, given the emotional situation.

"None other. The Donne fleet now belongs to a girl," she seemed to sigh as she said it. "I've been managing the firm for just over a month now. Dad always kept me filled in on his business, anyway. I've worked in the shipyard since I was a little girl."

"Well, Miss Donne," Jim answered. "My guess is that whoever this Red Jaguar is, he didn't know you were the sole heir; thus 'the Donnes.' My other guess is that the contract he mentions, doesn't refer to this letter as you may assume, but rather to a shipbuilding or shipping contract you may have received. Anything like that come up recently?"

"We're negotiating a contract with an independent British firm right now. But there's not much money in it. They're at war and can hardly afford materials. That's why they asked us to do it."

"And you were going to sign this contract?"

"My father was French, Mr. Anthony. And France appears to be on the same side of this campaign as Britain." There was a sudden strength to Severana's words.

Jim hoped America might still avoid entering the European conflict, so she wouldn't have to prove that strength. He looked thoughtful for a moment. "Miss Donne, would you be averse to staying in protective custody with us for a while? I'd like to make sure you're safe until we have a chance to get a handle on this thing?"

"Why, I would in fact be delighted, Mr. Jim Anthony." She smiled with both her eyes and mouth for the first time since entering the penthouse.

Jim smiled back. "Tom, we're going to The Tepee. Take the auto-gyro and go gas up the The Thunderbird. We'll follow along in the car after the courier arrives."

Tom was already up and putting his flight jacket on.

Chapter V
Lightning Strikes

High above the Catskills Jim Anthony's giant Douglass plane, The Thunderbird II, sailed though the air toward The Teepee. Tom had brought along an extra pilot to help fly her back, so he could stay with Jim at his secret hideaway along with Dawkins, Mephito and Severana Donne. The six of them were all gathered in the cabin, which looked more like a small efficiency apartment than the inside of a plane. Mephito sat on a parachute toward the rear, smoking a foul smelling pipe. Jim continued to go over the business files and police reports of the murder victims, while Dawkins served tea and sandwiches to everybody else. The new pilot continued to glance around nervously because nobody was at the controls—only a small black box.

The Anthony Robot, another of Jim's fantastic inventions, was piloting the transport plane to its destination, and a small red light would notify everyone when to jump out of the plane. The only way to get to the Tepee was to parachute in.

Gentry walked over to a metal table that was illuminated around the edges. Gazing at a transparent map of the country, and with the aid of a magnetic compass utilizing beams triangulated from Albany, Buffalo, and New York City, a pencil point of light showed their exact position.

"Five minutes," Tom announced, and everybody put on their pack except for the new pilot. "Five-hundred feet," Gentry said, pulling the lever to open the door. "The plane will circle until everybody has a chance to land," Gentry told the new man.

Mephito jumped first. He enjoyed the feeling of freefall and since he still had the eyes of a hawk, he had no problem sighting the gigantic net that acted as a landing zone for the hidden retreat. After he climbed out of it, he would switch on a series of landing lights for everyone else. Five minutes later a section of the forest appeared to light up.

Severana Donne was strapped onto Jim's chest in a special harness. Since she didn't know how to use a chute, the two of them would use a training model designed for two people. Counting down from three, they leapt out of the plane together. Dawkins made a sour face and jumped out on the next pass, followed by Gentry himself.

The new pilot gazed around the cabin with a horrified look on his face, as if he'd been abandoned. Thanks to the Anthony robot a pilot was really only necessary for take off and landing. Tom had informed their new employee he could man the controls himself, if the autopilot made him uncomfortable. From the look of things, The Thunderbird would have a human pilot long before it made it back to Manhattan.

"Oh my stars! I have never had such fun in my life!" Severana said, after landing in the net with Jim. "I am going to have to start building planes. Such excitement!" She pulled off her headgear and goggles and shook her hair down around her shoulders. Her shiny locks reflected sparks of red from the light and Jim caught himself lost in the aroma of her perfume. Dawkins came to her rescue, holding out a hand and offering to help her down.

The Tepee was the only property owned by the world famous detective where he could truly be alone if he chose. Discovered by his father years before, it had been originally planned for use as farming land—instead, when Jim had found it abandoned and overgrown years later, he decided to make it his personal sanctum. Mephito drove up through a screen of undergrowth in a tractor with a truck bed behind it. Everybody piled in. They crossed through dense forest on a nearly indistinguishable trail only to stop at an abandoned barn. The building seemed to be leaning, and so much paint had peeled off the gray wooden sides, it was hard to tell if the thing had ever been painted.

"…they leapt out of the plane together."

"So, this top secret Teepee is really a barn," Severana said. "And me without my overalls."

Jim picked the svelte redhead up effortlessly and carried her over a small bramble patch. "This is just the entrance," he said, pushing open a door that hung from one rusty hinge.

"Not much of one." Severana glimpsed around in the shadows as they walked across a cracked wooden floor with tufts of grass growing through it. "It looks like you may have your work cut out for you, Dawkins," she quipped.

"H'i fear you are right, Miss Donne. We 'aven't been here in h'ages. The place will need a frightful dusting."

Severana gave Dawkins a confused look as Jim touched the wall and a panel slid up in back of the dilapidated fireplace to reveal a small elevator. They rode down to the living room two at a time.

Jim let Dawkins give Miss Donne the nickel tour of the place, showing the vast underground mansion room by room. Severana was amazed by the trophy room in which sat both evidence from solved cases, and an array of plaques and statues from every sport one could think of. She offered to help Dawkins cook, but he pushed her out of the kitchen with a spatula and warnings about "those h'infernal h'electron tubes." Scared to set foot in the lab, she stumbled upon the library and grabbed a stack of recent National Geographic magazines. When she returned to the living room, Jim was sitting at a secretary's desk, wearing a pair of yellow swim trunks and going through copies of business files.

Severana watched, admiring his muscular physique before announcing herself. "Well, Mr. Anthony, you didn't have to dress up on my account."

Jim looked down at his chest as if he had forgotten what he was wearing. "Oh, sorry, Miss Donne. I didn't think you'd be too interested in going over evidence. Figured Tom would be attending to all your needs by now."

"Please, Jim, call me Severana. I haven't seen Tom since we got here. Can't trust those hotshot pilots, anyway. Besides, I was wondering if you were onto anything."

"Well, other than the notes, a sword cane and a poison cigarette butt, there doesn't seem to be that much evidence. Police are following up on the cane, but it was probably tailor made, possibly overseas—can't exactly track it back to the oak tree. As far as the poison, whoever signed for that probably used an alias. That leaves us with motive."

She curled up in a chair next to Jim, bending her legs and placing her heels in the seat. She wrapped her hands around her knees, rocking back and forth almost like a child. "All three of us were involved in some pretty big industry."

"Yes, big business. But whereas yourself and Hanlon were involved with manufacturing, Prescott was a banker. Mind you, he has owned stock in both Donne and Hanlon industries, but he hasn't so much as crossed paths with either of you in the last two years, businesswise." Jim gripped his chin between thumb and forefinger, staring up at the ceiling. Then his eyebrows came down as the shiny basalt glance of his eyes stuck on one side. He had an idea. He looked at Severana and picked up another piece of paper.

"You're onto something, aren't you?" she said.

"Nothing solid yet, just one of those feelings."

"Well, judging from what it took to get to this place you probably work better in solitude, so I'll leave you alone. Guess I'll go see what the flyboy's up to."

"He's probably tuning up the auto-gyro we use to get out of here. Get Dawkins to take you out there. By the way, Severana…"

"What?"

"I don't always work better alone." Jim smiled, and rang the bell to summon Dawkins.

Severana smiled back.

After fixing Miss Donne up with some clothing more suitable for the outdoors—a khaki skirt with a linen blouse and bush jacket—Dawkins pressed a panel in the living room wall and led Miss Donne up through the fireplace of the abandoned barn that served as The Teepee's tower. Stepping outside of the ramshackle barn, she was grateful for her new boots, too. There was no way the English valet could have carried her over the briar patch the same way Jim Anthony had. Dawkins switched on a flashlight and placed it in her hand the moment she realized how dark it was.

The cockney butler led her through a screen of undergrowth, across fern covered glades, under overgrown trees and giant boulders, then down the course of an ancient stream that had long since dried up.

She could just see the blades of the auto-gyro as they came into a partially camouflaged clearing. It was obvious Severana was enthused by the engines of transportation, and she had never seen an aircraft that could fly almost straight up and down before. All her attention was on what lie ahead and not what was going on around her. She neglected to notice the tripwire that popped up behind Dawkins from the forest floor.

A cord snapped around her ankle and the petite shipping magnate was suddenly whipped off her feet and dragged into the thick undergrowth of the forest. Screaming, her body jerked through the leaves as if some predator had caught her in its jaws. The tight sprung cord whipped her around a tree and she was dragged another ten yards through rocks and bramble.

Dawkins heard the commotion and turned around to shine his flashlight on the empty trail where Severana Donne had stood only a moment before. He spun the torch in concentric circles and, realizing she was gone, began to blow on the alarm whistle that he carried on a cord around his neck for just such an emergency.

Tom Gentry's head popped up from the engine cowling of the auto-gyro. You couldn't miss Dawkin's police whistle; and he wasn't the kind of guy that cried wolf. The ace trained agent pulled a .45 automatic out of the holster he wore on his belt and ran down the trail with the penlight he'd been using to view the engine in his hand. Rounding a blackberry bush he immediately saw Dawkins running off trail. Chasing the surprisingly fleet cockney through the woods, Gentry could see where the girl had been dragged through the leaves, through an array of twists and turns, more intricate than any snare he had ever seen before. When he looked back up—

Dawkins was gone!

The forest was still but the quiet was not peaceful. It was the moment of silence before the thunder. The lightning Mephito had warned them about!

Tom ducked as an arrow fired out the darkness, lodging in the tree next to him only inches from his head. He pointed the flashlight in the direction it had come from but the beam only melted into the shadows. Gentry couldn't fire blindly into the woods with Miss Donne and Dawkins out there. Cursing, he ran back in the direction of the auto-gyro to radio Jim Anthony.

The emergency walkie-talkie sitting on top of Jim's desk turned on automatically as Tom broadcast on the private wavelength. "Jim! Get out here! Something's happened to Miss Donne!"

Jim ran the tiny elevator to the barn express, and in seconds was running through the woods barefoot. If one had not known of Jim Anthony, this modern man of science, he would have thought he was looking at some feral creature of nature. For Jim bounded through the woods as if he were a part of it, his nostrils flared, eyes wide open like a wolf on the hunt. Branches cut at his shoulders, whipping him, as his leg muscles churned, carrying him over, above and around every obstacle in his path.

He had no flashlight, no radio, no weapon. But Jim Anthony was no normal man. He was also a Comanche warrior, trained from birth in battle, spirit and the ways of the hunt. Taught from a young age that the good we do in this life is passed on to all beings—two legged, four legged, finned and winged—he was a part of the wild. With both his wealth of inherited genetics and endless training, Jim Anthony could see in the dark like a cat, follow a trail like a hound and hear sounds inaudible to ordinary humans. He barreled through the forest, a force of nature, sliding on the balls of his feet to stop and turn on the exact spot of the trail where Severana Donne had been dragged into the underbrush.

Jim hurdled over a misshapen bush and, still running, noted every line in the soil where the snare had dragged the young lady through the woods. Stopping for only a moment where she had twisted around the trunk of a tree, Jim arched his head, sniffed the air, and loped off into the darkness, stopping at the edge of a fern covered glade.

Tom Gentry lay upon the ground unconscious, his flashlight beaming into the undergrowth where the remains of the rope from the snare had been stashed. Jim checked his pulse and headed another twenty yards in the dark to find Dawkins in the same condition. The medical care for his friends outweighed the need for the chase; unconsciousness for more than five minutes might cause brain damage.

Jim picked up Dawkins and carried him over to where Tom lay, gently slapping his face as the cockney valet began to moan. Within moments he had revived the both of them.

"Mr. h'Anthony!" Dawkins screamed upon waking. "Miss Donne 'as been h'apprehended!"

"Did you get a look at the man who took her?" Jim asked.

"He wore this frightful mask," Dawkins gasped between breaths. "With leaves or feathers h'all over it. So 'ard to see h'in this dreadful darkness."

A plane engine buzzed in the background.

"Small aircraft," Anthony said. "The Jaguar must have found somewhere to land and glided down, probably a biplane. We should have searched her clothing for some sort of homing beacon."

Tom stirred on the ground next to him

"Damnit, Jim! I never even saw him! One second I'm looking at Dawkins and the next, everything went black," Tom massaged the lump on his head. "Feels like he used a blackjack on me."

"Or a tomahawk," Jim said, shining the flashlight on the ground to reveal what looked like a relic from some ancient civilization.

Tom was about to tell Jim the idea of a tomahawk was loopy until he saw the thing. "Well, maybe it is a tomahawk? Doesn't look like anything I ever saw at a Wild West show though."

"No, it's not the Hollywood version, that's for sure," Jim said, holding the tomahawk up as he examined the odd snake's head carved on the stone. "Looks more like Aztec or Puuc-Mayan." Jim picked up the rope with his other hand, as Tom and Dawkins climbed to their feet, stopping for only a second to shine the light on something else he had seen. He bent over and picked it up, placing whatever it was in the pocket of his trunks. "Come on, we have to get back to the lab, radio the surrounding towns to be on the lookout. Then we're going to go over the evidence, figure out where the Red Jaguar's den is, and rescue Miss Donne—if we're not already too late."

Back inside Tom got on the radio while Dawkins prepared a drink to clear their heads. Jim was already in the lab. He'd gone over the rope in minutes, analyzing its makeup without any tools. If need be he'd give it a better investigation later, right now, time was tight. Jim knew he would have to check in the library for the origin of the bizarre tomahawk. Meanwhile, he had something in his pocket to check out.

The strange chunk of dirt the super-detective had stooped to pick up in the woods would have looked like a common dirt clod to the untrained eye, but to Jim Anthony it was much more. Jim's finely honed senses had somehow discerned, even in the dark, that the unassuming chunk of earth was somehow a major clue. Skillfully holding the tiny chunk of dirt with a pair of tweezers, Jim scraped the side of it with a razor blade, letting the grains fall precisely onto a glass slide and placing it under the microscope. He grabbed a pencil and notebook, computing his estimates of different soil types, minerals and a tiny speck of sea shell, into the percentages each part made up of the soil sample. He then pulled several files out of the cabinet in the corner, wrote down a series of numerals on the notepad, and looked up with the hint of a grin on his face. Jim wrote something in large letters on the bottom of the notepad, and stepped briskly out of the lab with the tomahawk in his other hand.

"I've notified every nearby town from Halletsburg to Brinley," Tom said to Jim as he passed. "Local sheriffs are all on the lookout. Radioed Trotter and they've got an APB out for her, too. Problem is this guy may not be headed back to New York."

"I don't think he is," replied Jim, heading for the library. He stopped right next to the chair where Miss Donne had been sitting earlier. His head jutted erect as if electrified. Every muscle in his body tensed. Jim Anthony's famed sixth sense was at work.

Tom Gentry's eyes narrowed and one side of his mouth turned upward. "You onto anything, Pappy?"

"Maybe. Remember those soil samples you were making fun of?"

"You mean those glitzy tubes full of dirt?"

"Yeah, pay more attention next time, because I think that research is about to pay off."

"OK, OK already! How can I help?"

Jim stared at the stack of National Geographic magazines next to where Severana Donne had been seated. "Go through those magazines—"

"You know, Jim, the girls in those things are never really my type."

Jim didn't even acknowledge the comment. "Look for anything that might involve shipping, banking, the Yucatan Peninsula, or islands off that coast."

Tom Gentry shrugged his shoulders, sat down, and started thumbing through magazines.

Once in the library, Jim reached high on the shelf for several volumes involving lost civilizations and archeology. On his way to the desk he pulled a volume on Central American Native Tribes out of the wall without even having to look. Ten minutes later he stepped back out of the library.

"Find anything, Tom?"

"Well, you want shipping, get the Shipping News. You want finance, get the Wall Street Journal. But, if you want the Yucatan Peninsula, I just spotted an article," he said, pointing to the table of contents in the magazine, and quickly flipping through the pages. "What about you? You got something?"

"The carving on the tomahawk is definitive of Puuc-Mayan culture, and our soil sample points directly to the Yucatan."

Tom's mouth opened wide. He seemed to want to say something for a second but couldn't get it out. He held the magazine pages open so Jim could see, and spoke two words with bated breath. "Chichén-Itzá."

The story's headline read, "Mayan 'Throne of the Red Jaguar' Discovered in Chichén Itzá Pyramid."

Chapter VI
Human Sacrifice

Late the next morning, The Thunderbird II soared above the thick forest of the Mexican Coast, sharply dropping in altitude as it reached the ruins of Chichén Itzá. Within minutes of spying the article, Jim Anthony, Tom Gentry, and Mephito had all boarded the auto-gyro and flown to the nearest airport to rent a plane. Flying immediately to New York, they re-hired their previous pilot and boarded the Thunderbird II, so they wouldn't have to stop for fuel on the way. Mephito had insisted on going; he kept calling the Mayans "the Old Tribe." Jim hadn't felt like arguing.

The hired pilot seemed a little more at ease this time around, letting Gentry know he was still marveling at the wonder of the Anthony Robot's automatic piloting ability. Jim graciously thanked him and told him to land the Thunderbird at the airport in Mexico City. With luck they could radio in for a pick up.

The light on the cabin wall glowed bright red, telling them it was time to jump. Tom watched the hired pilot to make sure he knew how to use the navigation table and, after donning separate knapsacks for supplies, they parachuted down to the ancient Mayan Village of Chichén Itzá.

Landing in the woods just to the southern edge of the ancient pyramid called the Castillo, Jim and Tom had been skillful enough to avoid getting entangled in the trees. Mephito had not been so lucky.

The old man had been warned not to let out with his usual war whoops as he dove down from the plane, so they could maintain the element of surprise. Tom had been worried that the old goat might start screaming for help from where he hung in the treetop. Jim seemed to have no qualms about it, stashing the parachutes in the bush and almost ignoring his grandfather, as the old medicine man unhooked his harness and swung to the trunk of the gigantic willowy tree. Tom held his breath as he watched Mephito navigate his way down through the branches with monkey-like agility. The aviator ran to the old man's side to make sure he was all right. Mephito jumped from the tree trunk and landed without making a sound.

"You know Itzá mean 'twisted speech.'" Mephito said. "Comanche speak different than any other tribe, twisted."

Tom's jaw hung open in amazement. The old guy was barely breathing hard.

"So you're saying the unique architecture of Chichén Itzá is because the Comanche were here?" Jim asked.

"Told you, old tribe," the medicine man said. Jim turned him around and gave the old man a gentle shove toward the Castillo.

"Twisted…" Tom muttered to himself.

Hiding themselves on the edge of the forest in the same manner Eduardo Valenzuela had only a week before, the band of men came as close to the north face of the pyramid as they could.

"I wish we had more time to prepare, map this out," Jim said. "But today is the summer solstice. Knowing how important astronomy was to the Mayans, I can only predict that bodes badly for Miss Donne."

"What do you mean?" Tom Gentry said.

"Ritual Sacrifice at noon," Jim said. "The Mayans practiced it religiously and, if his ransom notes even begin to hint at the insanity of The 'Red Jaguar'—he probably does, too." Jim pointed to the top of the pyramid. "The temple is up there. That's where they would have held such a sacrifice. Straight up the north face; he'll see us coming."

"Tom...worried the old goat might start screaming for help..."

Mephito nudged Jim's shoulder with his elbow and pointed at a small opening underneath the stairs on the north side of the pyramid. After that he slid the palm of one hand through a fist and made a walking motion with his fingers.

"Of course!" Jim said.

"What?" Tom was exasperated. Jim and the old man weren't even sweating in the heat.

"Mephito says we can use the stairs inside the pyramid." Jim had read the National Geographic article on the plane. The anthropologists had tunneled underneath the façade of the Castillo and found a second, earlier pyramid underneath. Climbing up the stairs of the interior structure was where they had found the throne of the red jaguar the article mentioned.

No one but Tom Gentry bothered to wonder how Mephito had known this, and Tom had given up on asking questions.

"We'll have to leave our tools here. Bring your flashlight and canteens. I'll go first, then Tom. Mephito, you stay here. I know you can handle yourself, but we can't take the chance of being seen running toward the site."

Mephito maintained his usual stoic expression.

Within seconds Jim Anthony was already at the excavation doorway, and motioning for Tom to follow. Tom peered up and through the foliage to make sure nobody was watching and then dashed for the doorway under the side of the steps. Clearing the entrance, a hand grabbed his shoulder. Tom raised his fist in the darkness, only to see Jim Anthony pointing the flashlight at his own face. Jim held a finger to his lips and Tom tried not to breathe too loudly.

The inside of the pyramid was dank and dark. Quite appropriate for an old tomb, Jim thought, as he motioned toward the interior steps with his flashlight. The two adventurers gingerly made their way up the ancient steps, until they came upon a human skull.

Jim knew before he had even picked it up that the skull was no relic. It was thin and had the brow of a modern man, without the sloped head that the Mayan's gave their young by tying a board to their head at birth. It also still had meat and blood on it. Jim grabbed Tom by the shoulder and whispered:

"It's got teeth marks on it. From an animal. Be careful."

Tom unholstered his gun.

Jim, already familiar with the layout of the temple, counted off the steps. At sixty, he stopped again and motioned for Tom not to move. Jim turned off his flashlight and went ahead. Tom kept his back to the wall, standing stiffly and firing a beam of light into the darkness at occasional intervals.

He kept glancing at his watch over and over. Tom felt like he had been standing here in the darkness all morning. He'd tell himself he wasn't going to look at his watch for at least one more hour, but then turn his flashlight back on to look at it, only to find maybe five minutes had passed. He shut out the light, and tried not to let the darkness get to him. If Jim Anthony could do this, so could he.

That's when he heard the cat purring. Only it was about a thousand times louder than your average house cat. It sounded more like a truck idling. Tom cringed against the wall, biting his lip, and forcing his eyes closed until he could stand it no longer. He opened his eyes and turned on his flash light. A black blur chased through the brightness and disappeared in the shadows. As Tom chased it with the flashlight's beam, the shadow became a living thing. A black jaguar sat on the steps directly in front of him. It growled.

Then pounced.

Tom already had his .45 in his hand, but he never got the chance to fire it. The very moment the jaguar leapt into the air, a force of nature jumped on its back. Jim Anthony.

The super-detective flew out of the darkness above, landing on the big cat's back, his weight and angle of deflection forcing it to the floor. The jaguar landed right in front of Tom, with Jim holding onto its back. The killer cat's growls tore through the air; its fangs so close Tom could smell its breath. But he couldn't fire the shot. Even with his own life in danger, Tom dared not risk the bullet striking his lifelong friend.

In one motion, Jim yanked his belt from around his waist like a sword from a scabbard, and whipped it around the jaguar's throat. Every muscle in his arms and back seemed to ripple and explode, as Jim Anthony strained himself pulling on both ends. The beast forced itself toward Tom; Jim Anthony's all too human muscle the only thing holding it back. Tom's finger tightened on the trigger.

Razor sharp claws pawed at the air, tearing through Tom's shirtsleeves like tissue—as the jaguar ever so slowly began to stand erect—and then fall backward! Jim had hold of the deadly black panther, and Jim Anthony was not letting go.

The big cat twisted in midair, swatting its deadly claws at Jim. Jim held on tighter and twisted along with it. The jaguar landed on all fours facing the darkness, Jim Anthony still on its back. Gripping both ends of the belt with one hand as if it were a horse's harness—Jim pressed the release on his belt and extended it. Holding the round, steel ball of the belt buckle, Anthony began to pummel the feline killer over the head with it, to little effect.

Flailing, the big cat scraped Jim against the wall and suddenly jumped, arching its back. Jim flew through the air, jettisoned from the panther's back. The fur between the big cat's shoulders stood erect in angry spikes, its growls echoing its fury. Tom's flashlight beam followed Jim through the air. Jim hit the steps of the ancient staircase, absorbing most of the blow with his shoulder, but the back of his head still bounced off the next step. He tried to sit up but, still dazed, he almost collapsed and rolled back down the staircase. The panther's eyes burned an emerald green through the darkness.

Jim lay on one side with his arm resting across his forehead as the big cat circled, growling, stalking Jim one minute, then Tom the next. The deadly beast stood back on its haunches preparing to launch instant death at Jim. When Tom fired two shots at its skull.

The panther turned, angry at Tom now, as if the bullets had merely distracted it. Gentry fired twice more, even though he knew he needed more firepower. Once again, the big cat flexed back on its haunches. Tom could see blood dripping from the black fur even in the darkness. He held his arm out stiff preparing for one last volley—as suddenly Jim leaped from the floor and jumped on the jaguar's back again! The big cat, startled by Jim's sudden sneak attack, seemed to be slowed by its wounds. Jim wrapped both arms around the deadly predator's chest and, grappling the beast in a full nelson, pulled the jaguar upright. This time there was no letting go.

"Shoot! Shoot it now! In the eye, Tom!" Jim ordered, holding the big cat sideways as high as he could. Tom emptied the .45's chamber into the beast's head. Both the panther and Jim collapsed to the staircase steps. Tom dropped his flashlight.

There was a moment of silence in the darkness, before the sound of the gun clattering off the ancient stone echoed in the chamber. Several minutes later there was a groaning sound as Jim pushed the big cat off the top of him. The sound of steps, briefly. And then a flashlight lit up, pointing at Tom.

"We're not going to really be able to clean those wounds till we get back outside," Jim said. "You going to be able to make it?"

Tom laughed hard and loud. It didn't matter anymore. He knew they had lost all element of surprise—but he was glad to be alive! He was still gulping air and he couldn't stop laughing. And Jim?—Jim wasn't even breathing hard. Tom laughed even harder. Damn, these Anthony men were tough. Jim began to laugh along with him.

He grabbed Tom by the shoulders and patted him on the back as he sat him down by the wall. Tom groaned in pain, and then caught his breath, before laughing again. Jim handed him the flashlight, then tore off one of the pilot's ripped sleeves using it to bandage Tom's arm. He then tore off Tom's other sleeve and fashioned a sling.

"What time have you got?" Jim asked the exhausted aviator.

Tom shined the flashlight at his limp arm. "Ten to noon."

"Not much time to stop a ritual sacrifice. Any more ammo?"

"Six more rounds."

"Load your gun, and wait here for me. I'll be back."

Tom Gentry tried to climb to his feet, and fell back against the wall. Anthony didn't even bother to tell his old friend that he would only slow things down. Jim bounded off into the darkness alone.

At the top of the ancient stairway, daylight burned leading up to the temple. By modern standards the temple was nothing more than a sacrificial altar, a square, stone slab that lay upon the rock rooftop of the pyramid. From the inside though, the light made it seem like a different world. A spiritual, mystical world of solid, unbreakable light and rigid, inflexible stone. Darkness and light. Life and death.

In the center of the stairs above, a man's silhouetted form stood holding a staff, illuminated from the sun behind him. An otherworldly knight errant in a headdress adorned with feathers, and the alien face of a jaguar god. A black feline creature of darkness paced back and forth in front of the man, rubbing itself against the thigh of his leg like an oversized housecat. The deep whirring vibration of the panther's purr suddenly stopped. The emerald eyes flared as the shadow cat roared its fury into the blackness.

"Give it up, Prescott. It's over," Jim Anthony said, walking up the ancient shadowed staircase. He was holding his belt like a lariat, spinning the steel, ball buckle in the air to one side.

"Benson Prescott is dead," the man said, stepping back into the light to reveal himself. "Prescott got soft. Died with the American Dream." He held out both arms as if to absorb the sun's power. "The Red Jaguar does not die."

"Everything dies eventually. Even the Mayan's." Jim took another step up. "The dreams are what keep us going."

"Easy for you to say, Anthony!" The Red Jaguar said, pointing the staff at Jim. "You were given everything!" He looked like a Mayan ruler confronting the accused.

"My dad had nothing when he came to this country. My mother's people lost everything."

"I'm not talking about your folks, Anthony! I'm talking about money!" Benson seethed with rage, his sunburned face flushing redder.

"You got greedy, Benson." Jim continued to step toward him. "Sold everything out for a short term profit. That's why your wife committed suicide. Or did you have her killed?"

"You dare talk that way to The Red Jaguar? A king?" Benson spiked his staff into the ground as he spoke.

Jim stepped up further. He could now see Severana Donne lying on the sacrificial altar in a torn blouse, unconscious or already dead. "My guess is you killed your wife." Jim took another step. "And when the businesses you'd invested in wouldn't follow you into your new scheme—and you couldn't pull it off alone—you decided to punish them."

"They were fools, Anthony! Just like you!" Benson looked down at his black jaguar pet and aimed his staff at Jim Anthony. "Kill! Sasha! Kill!"

The jaguar jumped from beside the altar and charged. This time there was no circling its prey, no growling, no thought at all except that of the predator. Its need to kill. To feed.

Jim Anthony stood steadfast. He stared directly into the eyes of the charging beast and pulled the circular, steel buckle of his belt into one hand. Jaws wide, fangs bared, the jaguar's growl cut the air as the killer cat pounced at Jim's throat.

Jim reared back as the beast's burning eyes were obscured by the slashing, killer teeth. He gripped the steel ball behind him and pressed the release button. As death launched directly at him, any normal man would have shied away by pure reflex. Any normal man would have tried to duck; to dodge the razor sharp fangs that flew through the air to end his life. Jim Anthony was no normal man.

With certain death only inches away, Jim grabbed the bottom jaw of the man-eating beast, and thrust his other arm down the panther's throat!

For a millisecond nothing moved. Jim stood solid, frozen, with his arm stuffed in the carnivorous beast's gullet as a crazed demigod raved on the steps above. Then he leapt back, the panther's teeth tearing at the flesh of his arms as he fell on his back.

The burning green eyes of the man-killer flared, not with fury, but with fear. The beast gagged, as if trying to growl but unable. A horrible retching sound emanated from it throat. The jaguar stepped backward. It was choking on Jim's distinctive steel belt buckle!

Horrible rasping sounds ripped the air as the beast continued to back away looking like some madman's version of a housecat trying to cough up a fur ball. Its eyes rolled in its head with the effort, as it reeled backward. Jim bounded back up the steps and grabbed the belt still hanging out of the beast's mouth, roping it around the big cat's jaws like a muzzle.

The panther's grunts and wheezes grew panicked sounding, as the black demon's eyes widened even more. The jaguar began to thrash for air, twitching and retreating toward the edge of the altar. The big cat now oblivious, Jim Anthony charged toward the beast and with a leaping kick, knocked it over the edge of the ancient Mayan pyramid!

The muted wheezing bleats of the panther lessened as it bounced down the steps of the Castillo, to be replaced with the sounds of the beast's slow death. Jim turned toward The Red Jaguar, fury in his eyes. Jim Anthony was angry.

"Money? You killed people because of money? Murdered? My God, man, we all lost money in the crash. My father—and me—were almost destroyed. But we never killed people!" Step by step, Jim Anthony closed in on the madman. "We didn't let money replace our soul!"

Prescott began to step backward. His knees were shaking. "You don't understand… you don't…"

Jim's eyes compressed to dark, bottomless slits. The fiery onyx of his retinas burned like the pits of hell. "I hope I never do."

Benson Prescott dropped the staff and continued to back away. "Now… now don't do anything rash here… I just wanted what was mine."

"It's over, Prescott. Give it up."

Prescott pulled Severana Donne upright on the altar, holding her with one arm, and placed a stone dagger at her throat.

"There's nowhere for you to go," Jim said.

"No… No… I'll kill her, Anthony!" Prescott's voice trembled. His face blanched. He tightened his grip on the unconscious hostage. There was a moment of silence as he tried to control his emotion.

Then, a growling sound pierced the air from behind him.

"Sasha?" Prescott said. "Sasha! She's still alive! You see, Anthony? You see? The Red Jaguar cannot be defeated!" Prescott dropped Severana back on the altar.

"No! Prescott, don't!" Jim said, as the madman slowly backed away.

"You can't defeat me! Nobody can! There's a new world order coming, Anthony. And people like you, you're weak!" Prescott smiled, his eyes not all there.

"No, Prescott—Jaguar—whoever you are. It's not what you think."

"You can't change destiny, Anthony! I was born to rule," Prescott turned away on his heel, completely ignoring Jim. "Come, Sasha, come! The Reich shall rule for a thousand years! And Central America is ours—"

Prescott's voice cut out abruptly as he saw the big cat charge over the top step of the pyramid. It wasn't Sasha.

"No! No! It's my desti—" The giant spotted jaguar, a native of Central America, pounced on the raving Prescott and seized his throat in its jaws. There was a cracking sound, and blood spattered the stone floor of the temple.

Jim stared as a red puddle formed and began to grow larger. The cat continued to chew. Then stopped, and looked up at Jim Anthony. Their eyes met, sizing each other up. Or perhaps sharing a message. Then the cat turned back to its meal.

Jim turned back toward the altar and picked up Severana in his arms. Her bosom raised and lowered beneath the torn blouse. She was still alive. Sharing one more glance with the rainforest's spotted emissary, Jim nodded his head to the beast before heading unhurriedly toward the inside steps.

Tom Gentry and Mephito stood silently just inside the shadows. The old man, sensing trouble, had defied Jim's orders and climbed inside to patch up the wounded aviator. They turned and walked down the ancient steps, taking their time.

"Hey, Pappy," Tom said. "I know now it was Prescott, 'cause I seen him, but how did you?"

"I honestly didn't even suspect until the plane ride here. I could see where he had cut out all his business dealings with companies like Donne Shipping and Hanlon's steel firm—but at first I just thought it was something that made the victims different. On the way here, though, I noticed all the companies Prescott was still invested in were doing business with the Germans. Then when I read the National Geographic article on the way here, it said the archeologists were professors at Elliot State University. Well, it just so happens, Prescott—who never went to college, and, never gave to a charity in his life—contributed almost thirty-thousand dollars to the university. Odd, don't you think?"

"I still don't get it," Tom said.

"As far as I can figure," Jim said. "Prescott lost his sanity—most probably after losing a lot more money than he gained after the depression. That would explain the erratic writing on the ransom notes at least."

"Yeah, but what was all that stuff about the Reich?"

"Prescott got his identity from his money. So, when the crash threatened his identity, he became a fifth columnist. I'm betting if we check out Elliot State we'll find some more of them there."

"So this guy—who I'm betting wasn't really doing the right thing to begin with—suddenly decides democracy doesn't work, and decides to become a fascist?"

"Exactly," Jim said.

"Wow, imagine the trouble we'd have if the U.S. was really at war with those guys?" The aviator said, squinting at the sudden light as they exited from the pyramid.

"Let's just hope it doesn't come to that."

The sun shined down on the four of them as they sat down on the ground by the steps. Tom and Mephito drank from their canteens as Jim gently splashed water on

Severana's face to revive her.

"How'd you know that jaguar wasn't going to eat you?" Tom said.

Jim opened his mouth, but Mephito held up his hand to silence him. "The cat—jaguar," Mephito said. "Jaguar carries messages from the living to the dead. Dead sent jaguar to protect us."

Severana's eyes began to blink and she moaned then opened her eyes. "Oh… Jim. We're all right."

"Yes." Jim smiled down at her. "Yes, we're all right." He looked up at the pyramid where those who had once sought too much power were now extinct. "The gods are watching over us."

THE END

Sticking My Writing Hand in the Lion's Mouth

Ask any pulp hound on the street about Jim Anthony, and the answer you'll usually get is: Jim Anthony? Doc Savage Clone.

I beg to differ. Mind you, I'm a huge Doc Savage fan, and yes, they were both scientific geniuses whose physical aptitudes made the rest of us look like the proverbial ninety-eight pound weakling. But the pulps were busting at the seams with scientific geniuses and physical marvels back in those days, and there were some pretty major differences between Jim and Doc.

The first and biggest major difference was, is, and always will be: girls. A lot of people think Doc didn't like girls but, once again, I can't seem to agree with anybody. My theory is that Doc was just shy and didn't know how to act around women. It was a logic versus emotion thing. Now Jim, he was a product of the "Spicy" line of pulps. Jim loved the ladies. There were always at least two gorgeous ones in every story. Jim was also the kind of guy a femme fatale could always pull a gun on because he was paying more attention to the other heat the women were packing.

Doc controlled his emotions—Jim got angry. Not just angry, but really, really angry. In fact by his third run-in with his arch nemesis, Rado Ruric, Jim got so mean he just planted a bomb on the guy and blew him up. I'm pretty sure Doc wouldn't have done that. So, while Jim may have been aimed at the Doc Savage audience, he seems like more of a tribute than a carbon copy. And, as you can see, there were elements of Superman and Tarzan in there, too. Me, I always thought of Jim Thorpe, All American athlete.

But, once again, "that Bell kid" is full of contradictions.

Plus, let's face it; there were two completely different Jim Anthonys. While all of Jim's stories were written under the pen name of John Grange, they were penned by at least two different sets of writers. Jim's first writer was Victor Rousseau. An English veteran of America's serialized Science Fiction pulps of the twenties, Rousseau was a product of Hugo Gernsback's Astounding school—in which the future would be perfect thanks to scientific wonders, the Boy Scout motto of "be prepared" always paid off, and those space age belt-communicators had yet to become annoying cell phones. Rousseau created the supporting cast you see in "Curse of the Red Jaguar" and a girlfriend, Dolores Colquitt.

A year or two later, along came the team of Robert Leslie Bellem and W. T. Ballard. Bellem and Ballard were both veterans of the Hardboiled and the Spicy detective pulps. Bellem was the creator of Dan Turner, Hollywood Detective. A great, if not horribly sexist character, Dan was the kind of guy that would plant a kiss on a dame's lips to find out if she was fooling around on her fiancé; obviously, if she didn't try to rip all Dan's clothes off she was true blue. Ballard's detective Bill Lennox appeared in Black Mask, the Holy Grail of hardboiled detective pulps. These guys knew their stuff.

So Jim Anthony went from being practically Flash Gordon, to a more hardboiled man of science, and all the supporting characters disappeared except for Tom Gentry. Tom went from being Jim's loyal companion to more of a skirt-chasing horndog. Damn that Dan Turner!

When offered the opportunity to write a Jim Anthony story by the fine folks at Airship 27 my first question was, "Which Jim Anthony am I going to write about?"

Being obviously conflicted and confused, I then answered by saying, "Why not do both?"

I had always wanted to do a Spicy pulp, and yet I found Jim Anthony: Hero much more intriguing than Jim Anthony: Manhattan Dick. So I kept the supporting cast, except for the girlfriend—because if you're writing a Spicy pulp the last thing you want to do is bring a sack lunch to a buffet. Then I told myself, "Self, I need a globe trotting adventure thing with some criminology thrown in and a couple of inventions that would've been cutting edge back in 1940."

My conflicted and confused self immediately contradicted, "Why don't we just start with the globetrotting adventure thing?"

I said, "Sure, but you have to come up with it."

I needed a villain, and for some reason the Egyptian God Anubis kept popping up. Great villain. He's a jackal, for cryin' out loud! He's also the "weigher of souls" which means he gets to pass judgement on everybody, which is a perfect thing for a sociopath to do.

The other trick I hadn't seen a pulp hero use yet was to stick their arm down the throat of a lion to keep it from eating them. Seriously, I read about this in a safari book eons ago, and you just know something like that would take nads of steel. About a year ago I read where some tribesman in Africa had actually done it. Not only did it keep him from being eaten, but he came out whole and became a local hero.

So here's my story, "Jim's going to stick his arm down a lion's throat in a pyramid where he's fighting Anubis."

So I looked some stuff up (which I advise other writers not do as it only makes things more complicated) and of course, as usual, history is confusing. The Super-Detective adventures all took place in 1939 to 1942 a period in which, due to too many episodes of The Rat Patrol as a kid, I was sure the Nazis were already running roughshod over Egypt. Turns out, there was a transition between Italy and Germany in there somewhere. Plus, there's the whole problem of airspace during a war, and I'm thinking even Jim Anthony can't just swoop in and machinegun everybody like The Rat Patrol did. I needed another pyramid.

So I remembered Chichén Itzá. Sure, it's a freakin' tourist trap now, but when I went to look up its history I found that in the thirties they were doing a great deal of digging around there. In fact, that's when they discovered there was a pyramid inside the pyramid. Then I saw the story of how they discovered "The Throne of the Red Jaguar." Ka-boom—Instant villain! Throne of the Red Jaguar almost became the name of the story, too. But it didn't sound quite pulp enough.

At the same time I'm learning all this stuff, I had already written what was going to be the opening that takes place at The Waldorf-Anthony Hotel. I quite liked opening with a beautiful babe in true Spicy fashion, but how was I going to introduce the villain? How could I get the reader to turn the page? Well, how about a murder scene, a massacre depicting ominous and foreboding things to come? Worked for me. Enter Eduardo Valenzuela, and then glue that part on the front of the story.

So, I got Jim in all his glory. I've got the cast. And I've got the villain. What's his motivation? Jim's a big businessman as well as a hero, so self said to self, "Why not rape the vault of history once again and use the premise of 'The Business Plot?'"

What's the business plot, you say? I don't want to get into politics too much here, but back in the thirties after the depression, there were quite a few people that weren't so sure our democracy was the best way of life. A lot of people leaned left. A lot of people leaned right. Some of those right leaners in Britain and in America were busted trying to arrange a corporate takeover, because they didn't want to stop doing business with Hitler. That's right, kids, these people would have sold a rope to the same man who wanted to put a noose around their neck. The newspapers in the UK dubbed this little venture "The Business Plot." Now, I'm all for free enterprise and everything, but…. Well, screw that. Needless to say, I decided to make the Red Jaguar one of those poor misguided business plotters.

So, I had hero, villain, motive, and sort of a plot in my head. As I barreled through, I had to remember to let Jim use his way cool belt, and I might as well admit right now that I've been wanting to use that cyanide cigarette trick for ages. I'll also admit that, given the chance, I just might use it again.

Going into this thing I once again had a problem with Jim being so damn perfect. Really, think about it, if I'd gone to school with Jim Anthony I probably would have hated the guy. But working on this yarn, I once again grew up as I grew more knowledgeable. When I started, I wanted to use some of Jim's Irish background, too. But as I came to know the character I realized the writers didn't use a lot of that. Maybe they just thought American readers wouldn't be able to identify with a Native American. Weird, huh? Also kind of funny, because a hundred years before Jim Anthony, the Irish weren't really looked at as being ideal Americans.

But hey, once again, past is prologue. Remember Jim Thorpe, All-American, attended the Carlisle Indian Industrial School, whose founding principle was to "kill the Indian and save the man." A lot of Native Americans weren't even given citizenship until 1924, just fifteen years before the Jim Anthony stories were written.

It's obvious to see that as I work on these stories I learn a lot. I love the pulps, as much or more than anything else I write. And it's nice that we can still embrace the heroic ideals that are given to us in the pulps. It's also nice to see how much we've grown, and use those same ideals to keep growing.

Now get out there and save the world, dammit.

B. C. Bell
10/10/2008

B.C. Bell - Inspired by illustrations in a Jimmy Olsen comic book, Airship 27 crew member B. C. Bell handed in his first story for editing at the age of six, and received a "B-" for misspelling the word "weird"—because he actually used that "I before E except after C" rule. He is author and illustrator of the now legendary Chicago mini-comic Dismental Tales, and is a past winner in the SFReader.com Annual Short Story Contest. He is also author of "The Gateway Machine" in Airship 27's Secret Agent X Vol. II. Bell is currently working on a future Airship 27 project and has just finished a science fiction, neo-noir novel that he's keeping under his hat until he gets an agent. You can read about his ongoing travails at www.myspace.com/noirishell.

AFTERWORD

by Ron Fortier

Finally it's here, after two long years and almost seeing it slip through our fingers. When I first started the ball rolling on Airship 27 Productions I put together a list of those pulp heroes we knew to be public domain and that we could play with. At the time, I had no idea who or what Jim Anthony Super-Detective was. After a little research, his history became clearer and I knew this would be a fun character to bring back from those long forgotten pulp archives.

The next step was to find writers to do new stories and the very first one to sign for this project was my pal, Andrew Salmon. At that time, Andrew had never written a pulp story and he dove into this assignment with his typical enthusiasm; something I've since become quite familiar with. In a few short weeks he had turned in his story and I was confident it would soon see print.

But twists of fate derailed us unexpectedly and for several agonizing months, *Airship 27 Productions* simply ceased to exist. I advised Andrew to submit his story elsewhere and he did so. I was naturally upset we would not be the ones to publish his first pulp tale, but at least it would get published. That was the important thing.

Since I am most certainly not a seer, how was I to know that within months our fortunes would change once again, this time for the better? Suddenly, it seemed we were back, stronger and better due in total to Michael Poll and Cornerstone Books Publishing. Rob and I began cranking up the production wheel and soon new *Airship 27 Prod.* titles were once again being released. As each new book hit the market and our presence began to be felt among the pulp community, I started dusting off those old projects we had been forced to put on hold, including *Jim Anthony Super Detective.*

By then, Andrew had written several other pieces for us including a *Secret Agent X* adventure that appeared in our deluxe reprint of *Secret Agent X – Voume One.* He then brought us his sci-fi thriller, *The Light of Men,* co-wrote *Ghost Squad – Rise of the Black Legion,* with yours truly and most recently did his second *Secret Agent X* for our *Volume Three* of that series. When he learned that we were taking up Jim Anthony again, he immediately asked if he could still be a part of the project. As it turned out, two years later, that other publisher had yet to publish his story. Andrew went to them, explained the situation, got the story back and handed it to us a second time. When he did so, I made a silent vow to myself that come hell or high water, this time it would see print.

Thanks, Andrew, for your faith in us, and for becoming a major part of *Airship*

27 Prod. over the past few years.

This first issue of what will be an on-going series, also features the work of another *Airship 27* veteran, Erwin K. Roberts, although this marks his first time in print for us. Roberts has been a professional writer for many years and has a deep, abiding love for pulps. He and Andrew are joined by B.C.Bell, who marks his second appearance with us. Bell had contributed a new story to our reprint edition of *Secret Agent X – Volume Two*. He's a solid writer with a knack for purple prose, as is quite evident in his new Jim Anthony adventure. He also knows a bit about the character's history, as his essay shows. Norman Hamilton, a regular contributor to *Airship 27 Prod.* was impressed with Bell's piece and made sure to focus his own article on other aspects of the character's history.

Lastly, we tip our pulp fedoras to the artists who have made this a truly beautiful book. Chad Hardin, a DC Comics regular, provided us with his gorgeous and traditional Jim Anthony cover. When Rob and I first saw it, we were delighted and awed. This young man has so much talent. We hope to keep him aboard the airship for as long as possible. We also welcome Portuguese artist Pedro Cruz. One of our writers made me aware of Pedro's work on-line and suggested he was the type of artist who would enjoy our over-the-top action material. Sure enough, one letter was all it took to get Pedro on board and start producing his wonderful interior illustrations that perfectly capture the fun and thrills of the stories themselves.

As always, thanks so much for your patronage of this and all our *Airship 27 Prod.* titles. In these economic hard times, we are sincerely grateful for your continued support of our efforts. The year 2009 is off to a rollicking start with tons of great new books due for release in the weeks and months ahead; *Dan Fowler G-Man, The Masked Rider Wild West Tales, Black Bat Mysteries, Ravenwood – Stepson of Mystery, The Green Lama* and *Sherlock Holmes Consulting Detective*. Those are just a few of the titles we have planned. And *Jim Anthony SuperDetective Volume Two* is already in the works.

You can find all our titles on-line at (http://www.gopulp.info) or at all major book outlets. Till next time, from Hangar 27, go out and read a pulp book. There's nothing like a great pulp adventure.

Ron Fortier
3/12/2009
Somersworth, NH
(www.Airship27.com)
(Airship27@comcast.net)

JIM ANTHONY
SUPER-DETECTIVE

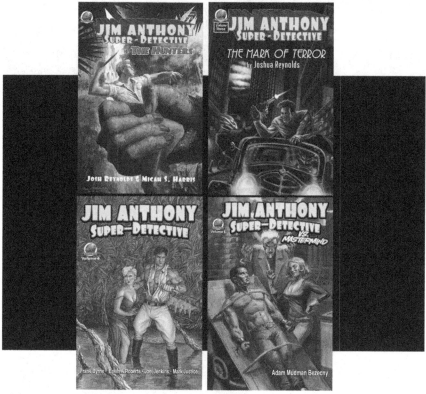

Airship 27 Productions is thrilled to present the all new adventures of one of pulpdom's most cherished two-fisted action heroes, Jim Anthony Super-Detective. Half Irish, half Comanche and all American, Jim Anthony is the near perfect human being in both physical strength and superior mental intellect. He's a scientific genius with degrees in all the major fields. Operating from his penthouse suite, which also houses his private research laboratory, he ventures forth into the world at large as a champion of justice, a modern knight righting wrongs and defending the helpless.

Follow the "super-detective's" all-new adventures in these volumes written by today's best New Pulp Authors.

For availability go to: Airship27Hangar.com

Pulp Fiction for a New Generation!

141

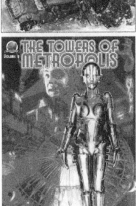

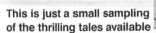

Made in the USA
Las Vegas, NV
13 December 2023